ALL THE LIES

LIES & TRUTHS DUET BOOK 1

RINA KENT

To those who never give up.

AUTHOR NOTE

Hello reader friend,

If you haven't read my books before, you might not know this, but I write darker stories that can be upsetting and disturbing. My books and main characters aren't for the faint of heart. I don't do trigger warnings, but if you need one, then my books are probably not for you.

If you, however, have read my other books, get ready for another twisted journey with complicated characters and intense passion you all love to hate.

All The Lies is the first book of a duet and is NOT standalone.

Lies & Truths Duet:
  #1 All The Lies
  #2 All The Truths

Don't forget to Sign up to Rina Kent's Newsletter for news about future releases and an exclusive gift.

I'll bow.

I'll break.

I'll pay for what I've done.

Problem is, I don't remember what I've done, but I have a clue.

There was a fire.

A dead girl.

And I was there.

BLURB

When lies become the truth.

My name is Reina Ellis.
Popular.
Beautiful.
Untouchable.
Problem is, I remember none of it.

His name is Asher Carson.
Gorgeous.
Silent.
Dark.
Oh, and my future husband.

He has three rules for me:

PLAYLIST

Every Breath You Take – Chase Holfelder

Amsterdam – Coldplay

Heartbeat – Point North

Breakeven – The Script

Sinner – Deaf Havana

Into The Dark – Point North & Kellin Quinn

¿ - Bring Me The Horizon & Halsey

Prom Queen – Molly Kate Kestner

Admit Defeat – Bastille

Save Me – XXXTENTACION

In Between – Glass Tides

Yours – Jake Scott

Just Exist – Eliza & The Delusionals

It's Ok Not To Be Ok – Little Hurt

Dig – Arrested Youth
You Know That – No Love For The Middle Child
Roses – Soleima
Scream – SAINT PHNX

You can find the playlist on Spotify.

CHAPTER 1 - R

I THREAD my fingers through her identical ones and smile.

It's the first time I've let go of my shackles and every weight that used to hold me down.

My family.

She's my family.

We're the same.

Same strawberry blonde hair, although hers is shorter. Same skin that appears tanned but isn't. Same huge blue eyes that mirror the deep ocean and the vast sky.

We might have lived apart, but we're still the same.

We still look at each other like we're mirrors, like we're halves split into two different bodies.

From today onward, my life will be different. I've

finally found this peace, and I'll do whatever it takes to protect it.

We sit on an old bench in a cottage. It's humid with the scent of pine and grass drifting through the half-broken window. The forest surrounding us feels like a protection against the outside world.

This is our haven.

Our sanctuary where no one can find us.

It brings back memories from the times when Reina and I used to hold each other and hide.

Back then, we made no sound. We barely breathed.

We have a lot of catching up to do. I can't wait to hear all about how she's been all these years.

A crunching sound of boots on the ground filters in from outside the cottage.

We jerk upright at the same time. Our hands become sweaty, and the peace from earlier evaporates into thin air.

"Are you expecting someone?" I sound as spooked as I feel.

She nibbles on her bottom lip, her body shaking. "You know, I told you…"

"What?"

"I run with a bad crowd, Rai."

I grab her shoulders and bore my eyes into hers. It's strange to stare at myself. "We'll go to the authorities.

No one will hurt you anymore, Reina. We'll be together like we promised."

She holds out her pinkie, eyes shining with unshed tears. "Pinkie swear."

I laugh at the childish gesture and grab her pinkie with mine. "You're supposed to be twenty-one, but whatever. Pinkie swear, you little girl."

"Hey! I'm five minutes older than you."

"Yeah, whatever."

A bang sounds on the door. Both of us flinch.

My heart pounds against my ribcage so hard, it's the only sound I'm able to hear.

Thump, thump, thump.

Reina pulls me by the sleeve of my jacket, a slight tremor in her hand. "You need to run."

"No. I'm not going without you. Not again."

She shakes her head. "Now that Grandpa is gone, if they find out about you, it's game over. You have to go, Rai."

I shake my head frantically, holding on to her with all my might. "I won't lose you after finally finding you."

"You won't. We'll always find our way back to each other. After all, we're…"

"One."

We say the last word together.

She nods, eyes hardening again. "Remember when we used to play hide and seek with Mom?"

"I do. We'd go in different directions to distract them."

She grins. "Diversion."

"Okay, okay," I mutter with resignation I don't feel.

The last thing I want to do after reuniting with Reina is to part from her again, but I have to believe we'll find each other like we always do.

"I'll take the window, you take the door."

I pull her in for a quick hug, my chest constricting and full of all types of chaotic paranoias. "I'll meet you outside."

"I love you, Rai." She ruffles my hair.

"I love you, too, Reina."

The moment I let her go, my heart squeezes so tight it nearly bursts.

I watch my sister hop up and climb out the window. She's so agile, which is no surprise considering where she lived all this time.

We'll change that. She'll get her fresh start.

With one last look, I sprint out the back door.

When we were with Mom, Reina and I learned something important.

Never look back.

If you don't look back, you run faster.

If you don't look back, no one will catch you.

I sprint through the woods, the smell of earth and the forest filling my nostrils.

Dirt smudges my white shoes and my breathing deepens as I cut across the distance. I search sideways for a place to hide then notice my bracelet is gone.

No.

I come to a halt and break my own rule.

I look back.

Flames devour the old wood of the cottage we escaped minutes ago. Smoke and fire erupt in the middle of the forest.

Someone dressed in black trousers and a hoodie drags Reina back into the cottage as she fights and claws at his hand. Masculine hand. Tattooed hand.

My heart stammers and my legs weaken. I take a step forward then stop when she meets my gaze and shakes her head.

She's pleading with me to remember our vow from all those years ago.

If one is caught, the other needs to run.

I made that mistake before. I ran away without looking back.

That day, I lost my only sister.

But I'm not a kid anymore. We're not running away with Mom.

This time, I'll save her like she once saved me.

Energy buzzes into my veins as I charge forward. My fists are balled by my sides. My hair is in disarray around my face, the blonde strands sticking to my temples with sweat.

I'm only a short distance away when Reina shrieks, "Noooo!"

Something hard and heavy hits the back of my head. I fall to my knees with a thud.

Black stars form behind my lids as they flutter closed, filling with tears.

Through the small slit, I stare at the burning cottage. Her loud, pained screams filter from the inside. The sound is raw and…lethal.

"R-Reina…" I croak, reaching out a weak hand before it falls limp in front of me.

All sounds disappear.

Reina is no longer screaming.

No longer shrieking.

No longer…fighting.

A sob lodges at the back of my throat as darkness swallows me whole.

CHAPTER 2 - G

DECIMATION IS AN INTERESTING PROCESS.

It starts with one crack. Then two. Then everything crumbles and falls apart.

The art lies in starting that first crack. It has to be precise and to the point.

It has to be unmistakable and with the purpose to hurt.

Better yet, it has to come out of nowhere. Victims are easier to handle when they're ambushed, when their world is flipped upside down in a fraction of a second.

Today, a process of decimation has started.

Reina's life is now mine to own.

Mine to torture.

And mine to finish.

CHAPTER 3 - REINA

One week later

Help!
Someone help!
Please help me!
"No one will help you, monster."

I CRACK my eyes open and wince. The back of my head feels as heavy as metal.

Constant beeping. Smell of bleach and coffee. Classical music.

The moment blinding white light penetrates my eyelids, I screw them shut again.

I'm obviously at the wrong place in the wrong time.

Isn't there a song about that?

"Reina?"

Someone's fingers force my lids open and shove another blinding light into my line of sight. My pupils burn with the intrusiveness of it.

"Miss Ellis, can you hear me?"

"Reina, honey, open your eyes."

Reina? Who the hell is Reina?

There's something wrong about that name. Completely freaking wrong.

Wrong place. Wrong time. Wrong name.

The voices continue drifting in and out around me. Someone calls me Miss Ellis. An older voice keeps calling me Reina. And then there's another presence, someone I can't quite pinpoint.

His masculine voice is like a dark forest in the middle of a starless night. It's deep and rough around the edges as if all the ruthlessness in the world has been injected into it. It's scary how much a voice can relay.

It's almost crippling how much a voice can become a subject of nightmares.

All the other voices keep asking if I'm fine and telling me to open my eyes, but not him.

No.

The nightmare voice is calm, unlike them. He's composed and speaks with chill-inducing purpose. "Wake up, monster. You don't get to die just yet."

His words register slowly. It's my brain. The useless thing understands with delay.

My heart thumps loud and hard at the threat in those words, at what he called me.

Monster.

This can't be true.

It's a dream—no, a nightmare. Soon, it'll all end and I'll go back to normal.

Only…what's normal?

I'm not Reina or Miss Ellis or whatever the hell they keep calling me. I'm someone else.

I'm…I don't know who I am. Reina is familiar, but it isn't me.

Wrong. Everything is so damn wrong.

My trips in and out of consciousness become exhausting. It's like I'm playing hide and seek with the darkness; only I'm not sure if I'm running away from it or sprinting toward it.

There's something enchanting about the darkness… a push, a pull. It's like a haunting lullaby with ever-changing lyrics.

I keep trying to avoid the blinding light and the voices. So many damn voices surround me like audible torture.

They keep heightening and magnifying, and there's no way I can stop them from assaulting my senses.

They're like an unreachable itch beneath the skin.

Then, one day, when I think I'm about to go crazy, my eyes open. Or maybe my brain finally catches up to that fact.

The back of my head aches, and so do my limbs. It's as if someone beat me up with a baseball bat.

Wait...is that what happened?

The blinding light renews the urge to close my eyes again, but I don't. I keep them wide open—as wide as I can considering the circumstances.

If I close them again, I might never open them back up. I'll return to the hide and seek game with the darkness.

I'll go mad for sure.

My surroundings are blurry. Mismatched shades of white become more and more defined the harder I focus. A headache lodges firmly at my temples the more I try to make out my immediate environment.

White walls. The same bleach smell. No classical music or coffee this time, which probably means the man with the older voice who used to talk to me isn't here anymore.

"Miss Ellis, you're back," a soft voice calls from beside me before an Asian woman's kind face comes into view.

Her black hair is tied into a bun underneath her

white cap, and some wrinkles surround her pulled brown eyes.

She checks something on the machines around me and nods to herself with a smile. "I'll call Dr. Anderson. Do you need anything?"

I attempt to shake my head, but the stabbing pain at my nape stops me.

When I say nothing, she asks, "How do you feel?"

"Like hell," I grunt in a scratchy, barely alive voice. "Have I been in hell?"

"You've been so lucky, dear. You gave us a fright." She smiles and leans in to whisper, "Your fiancé hasn't left your side the entire time."

I have a fiancé?

No, that can't be right. I don't have a fiancé. I don't have anyone.

Wrong. Everything is just so wrong.

"It's rare to see that kind of devotion in college kids these days."

College.

Okay, so my name is Reina Ellis, I'm in college, and I have a fiancé.

Did I mention *wrong*?

None of this adds up in my brain…or is it still trying to keep up with reality?

When I raise my eyes again, the kind Asian nurse

isn't speaking to me anymore. Her attention is on something—or rather, someone—over my head. "Congratulations on your fiancée's recovery, Mr. Carson."

"Thank you."

My spine locks and a shiver shoots down my back, covering my entire body.

The rough, deep voice with the slight huskiness.

The *nightmare* voice.

The one who called me a monster and…something else.

There was something else, but I've forgotten what it was.

Hell, I've forgotten a lot of things.

I don't even remember why I'm here, my age, or my damn name.

Everything is a blur. It's like I can reach the answer, but the moment my fingertips brush against it, it turns into fog.

The nurse says something else, but I miss her words —again, my brain has trouble keeping up. Everything happens too fast, like in some futuristic show.

Wait, are we in a Black Mirror *episode?*

How do I even know *Black Mirror* and not my own life?

The last thing I focus on is the door hissing open then closed behind the nurse.

My throat chooses this exact moment to become scratchy and sour. I glance to the side, searching for water.

A bottle sits on a small table, and I reach my arm out to grab it.

Huge mistake.

Something in my right shoulder pops and pain explodes in my muscles. I groan and bite down on my lower lip to stifle the sound.

Pain is temporary. Pain is temporary.

Mom's words echo in my head like a mantra.

I blink twice. I remember having a mother.

That's the first thing I've remembered since waking up in this sterilized room.

"Look who returned to the world of the living."

My movements freeze as that same voice echoes around me. I forgot he was still in the room in the first place.

I don't hear the sound of footsteps or feel him approaching.

The attack is silent and fast. One moment I'm thinking the nightmare is a reality, and the next, a broad, tall figure looms over my bed.

You know that color a tropical forest has when it's raining heavily? That's the color of his eyes. Dark green, almost black.

Harsh.

Emotionless.

There's something about those eyes that pushes me into a high-alert mode.

I want to run.

I want to hide.

But I can't. Something tells me it's not only because of my physical injuries. I'm unable to run from *him.*

He's wearing a simple white T-shirt and a black leather jacket along with dark jeans. His hair is the color of a moonless night with a bluish hue. It's short on the sides and long enough in the middle to be tousled.

The straight, chiseled jawline and the thick brows give him a fatally attractive edge—the kind serial killers have.

His broad shoulders and lean waist increase the intimidation of his already dark exterior tenfold.

Well, the physique is understandable. After all, he's an athlete who slaves at the gym and practices constantly.

Wait—how do I know that?

His upper lip lifts in a cruel smirk as if he injected all the shadows in it. "I knew you would come back."

Unlike the nurse, he doesn't seem relieved about

that. No. He's like a hunter who's closely observing his prey right before the attack.

A lightning strike right before the thunder.

The click of a gun right before the shot.

Suddenly, I wish I'd surrendered to the darkness of unconsciousness. That type of darkness is better than this one.

Don't they say some monsters are better than others?

His hand reaches out for me and I instinctively push against the pillow. Pain explodes in my head and my upper shoulder, but I don't stop.

I need to stay away from his hold.

Run.

Run!

My instinct has caught up with my slow brain and is now shouting at me to get the hell out of here.

In my condition, it's impossible to move a muscle, let alone run.

I glance behind me at the emergency call button. Maybe if I ask the kind nurse, she can remove him from my side. Maybe someone can help me.

Because I need help right now.

I can feel it in my bones and taste it on my tongue.

He releases a tsking sound that gets past my ears

and embeds under my skin. "No one will save you. It's just you and me."

Like doom coming closer, his hand reaches for me, and he clutches my chin between his thumb and forefinger.

It's a soft touch, so soft it shocks my warm skin. The emotionless look in his dark eyes is anything but gentle, though. A sadistic smirk lifts the corner of his lips.

A shudder emerges from deep within my soul.

It's the look of someone out to destroy, to maim and mutilate—and he'll do it all with a smile on his face.

"L-let me go." It's the pleading of the dying, my voice. The last murmur of the dead.

His grip tightens on my jaw until I wince. "That's not how it works. Remember the rules?"

"W-what rules?"

"Break willingly and I might let you collect the pieces."

My heart thunders until the machines erupt with sound. "What—"

My words are cut off when he leans closer until his breath tickles along my skin. Another involuntary shudder slides down my spine, and goosebumps form along my limbs.

I don't know if it's because of fear, or if it's something else.

This close, he's even more fatally gorgeous and dangerous. A flicker of connection grips hold of me.

I know him from somewhere, but *where*?

He runs his tongue from under my eye to the corner of my lip. Something violent and out of control takes over my body, and more goosebumps erupt.

I stare at him with trembling lips.

"Welcome back to your custom-made hell, monster."

THUMP. Thump. Thump.

My heart does this weird thing, beating in and out of sync, as if it doesn't know what to do.

There's so much sadism in his eyes.

So much…grudge.

The way he watches me intently with those rainy forest eyes is close to being cut open and left for dead.

Maybe I already died and crossed over to hell, and this is my torturer.

Otherwise, why the hell is he calling me a monster when I don't know him?

No—I don't *remember* him. I most definitely know him from somewhere.

But where?

According to what the nurse said, he's my fiancé. For some reason, that sounds wrong.

He's not my fiancé. He's someone more…sinister.

I try to lift my head. Pain shoots down my nape and snaps to the front.

Whimpers leave my lips as I try to tamp down the agony. I bite my lower lip to keep the sound from escaping.

No one will witness my weakness, least of all this stranger.

He watches me intently, his face impassive other than a slight twitch in his upper lip.

Wait…

I meet his dispassionate gaze and focus on the slight curve in his lips. My brain might be slow in keeping up, but I recognize that look.

It's pleasure, sadistic and twisted.

He's enjoying seeing me hurt. He's watching my aching shoulders and the trembling of my lips like he's in a competition and they're his prize.

He likes my weakness and my pain.

He likes my suffering.

Help.

Someone help me.

A voice from my dreams—or nightmares—whispers in my head. That voice is so similar to mine.

Who the hell did I ask for help from before? I don't like asking for help. I might not know my name or my damn age, but I know I don't like showing vulnerability that way.

The door hisses open, cutting off my connection with the asshole who called me a monster. He releases my chin and steps back as if he wasn't suffocating me not two seconds ago.

The kind nurse from earlier returns with a skinny, black doctor who's wearing frameless glasses.

The asshole clutches my wrist and sits by my side, holding my hand in his. Shock ripples through me at how soft, yet cold his touch feels.

How can a touch be so gentle and yet so…cold?

It's like I'm being held by a freezer.

His attention falls on the doctor and he smiles. There's something curious about that smile. It's not exactly fake, but it's…dead. Lifeless, just like his touch.

"Dr. Anderson." He speaks in such a polite, calm way. It's completely different from the asshole from earlier. "How is my fiancée doing?"

I stare between him and his hold on my hand. No, I can't be the fiancée in this tale. This fucking jerk can't be my future husband. I'd really feel sorry for myself and my poor choices if that were the case.

I mean, come on, first I don't remember my name,

then someone calls me a monster, *and* that same someone turns out to be my freaking fiancé?

A girl can only take so many shocks all at once.

"Miss Ellis." The doctor smiles in that polite but distant way. "How do you feel?"

"In pain?" I don't know why it comes out as a question.

I swear Mr. Asshole's lips twitch. In amusement or in sadism, I don't know.

Dr. Anderson and the nurse do a thorough examination, including checking my pulse and my temperature. He also puts that light thingy in my eye. Now I know who was bothering me in my sleep.

"Do you remember your name?" he asks.

"It's…" The name hovers at the tip of my tongue, but it's like I can't reach it. "I d-don't know."

Sure, I heard the name Reina Ellis before and after I regained consciousness, but I don't relate to that name.

That name is wrong.

So I choose not to say it.

The doctor scribbles something in his notepad and continues asking me about what year it is, what country we're in, what state, who the president is, etc.

I answer all of them in a beat. I count to twenty. I recite the alphabet.

When he asks me again about my name and my age, I freeze.

The entire time, the monster who called *me* a monster doesn't let go of my hand. His presence is an unyielding, dark entity, all-powerful and non-negotiable. The stabbing pain at the back of my head pales in comparison to how constant he is.

Dr. Anderson nods as he goes through a pad in his hand. "We thought we'd lose you to the vegetative state, Miss Ellis. You're lucky."

Lucky? Is he blind? Can't he see the looming presence by my side? It's like he's waiting for the doctor and the nurse to leave so he can pounce on me.

Cut me open.

Eat me alive.

I try meeting the nurse's gaze and asking her for help, but I don't get the chance.

Or more like, the asshole blocks my communication. Whenever I try to catch her eye, he tightens his hold on my hand, making me wince.

Motherfucker.

"What…what happened to me?" I finally ask the question that's been playing in my mind since I opened my eyes.

"Blunt-force trauma to the head." Dr. Anderson's

brows soften. "A hunter found you in the forest near the edge of town."

My nose scrunches. "What was I doing in the forest?"

"That's what I want to know, Reina." Those deep green eyes are so close I can feel the malice rolling off my skin and seeping into my bones. "What were you doing there? Were you thinking about leaving Blackwood?"

I try to pull my hand from his, but he grips me harder, disallowing my release. "I...I don't remember."

Then it dawns on me. *I don't remember.*

And it's not only about why I'm at the hospital or the asshole holding my hand or even my name.

It's everything combined. I have no recollection of my entire life prior to waking up here.

Oh, God. Oh, no.

Is this some sort of a telenovela?

Dr. Anderson nods. "Short-term amnesia is common in such cases. Now that the swelling has gone down, the memories should trickle in eventually."

"Swelling?" My eyes widen.

"Yes." The doctor flips through his file. "When you first arrived, there was swelling caused by blunt-force trauma. It's the cause of your two-day coma, but we've been monitoring it and gradually reducing it, and we've succeeded. As I said, you're young, and short-term amnesia isn't uncommon."

"You…you don't understand," I croak. "I don't remember anything about myself."

Dr. Anderson nods with thoughtfulness. "All tests came back with no problems, but we'll run one more MRI and CT scan to make sure. You have basic common knowledge, and everything else will trickle in."

"What if it doesn't?" I ask, voice spooked as if I were out in a dark winter night.

"Then it'll be a case of retrograde amnesia."

"And I can't be cured of that?"

"The brain is a complex organ, Miss Ellis. We still know so little about how it works. Unfortunately, there's still no cure for amnesia, but if you return to your normal life and surround yourself with friends, family, and familiar items, especially scents, it might help in regaining your memories."

Might.

As in even the doctor doesn't know how the hell I go back to normal.

But then again, what is normal?

Surely it doesn't include the asshole holding my hand or the pain pulsing at the back of my head.

"Your guardian should be here soon, but it's better if you rest," Dr. Anderson says before he leaves.

I have a guardian, but I'm in college. How does that work exactly?

"How...how old am I?" I ask the nurse.

"Twenty-one, remember, Rei?" the asshole on my right says with a sickening smile that doesn't even come close to reaching his eyes.

It's fake.

He's fake.

There's nothing genuine about him. I must've been out of my damn mind when I accepted his proposal.

That is if he ever proposed in the first place. For some reason, I think I just ended up with him and that's it.

That's even scarier.

"No, I don't remember," I hiss. "Have you heard a word I've said? I just told the doctor I don't remember my life."

He raises one thick, perfect eyebrow. "Huh."

Just one word. *Huh.* What the hell am I supposed to do with that?

"You're just distressed, Miss Ellis." The nurse smiles down at him with so much affection, like he's her son or something. "Asher has never left your side since you were admitted. He's been so sweet."

Asher.

Asher…

The name doesn't ring a bell, but the fact he's been by my side… I watch him again, trying to get a different feel for him.

No. Nothing.

He's just the nightmare voice and the one who called me a monster.

Those sinister eyes meet mine as he speaks to the nurse with a disgusting friendliness. "She's the only one I have. Isn't that right, Rei?"

Rei.

Fucking Rei?

He doesn't get to give me a nickname after he called me a monster. How can he say them both and sound so convincing and…frightening?

He doesn't get to act like the perfect human being in front of other people when I can sense him plotting my demise.

The nurse almost swoons at his words.

My shoulder blades knot together as a strangling fear closes my throat.

Wrong. Everything is so freaking wrong.

The nurse smiles as she injects my IV with something. "You're a lucky girl, Reina."

Would everyone stop saying that? How can she not

see the threat looming over me like damnation? It's pouring onto my skin like acid.

And for crying out loud, would everyone stop calling me Reina? That's not my name.

But again, if I don't remember my name, what makes me so sure it isn't Reina?

I grab the nurse's hand as she retreats. This is the only chance I'll get to put a stop to this, and I won't miss it for the world.

"Is something the matter, dear?" the nurse asks with a kind expression.

"H-help me. He's going to hurt me."

Asher's grip on my hand turns painful, but even if the nurse looked down at our joined fingers, she'd only see his thumb moving over the back of mine as if caressing it.

When he speaks, it's in pure concern. "Is it your assailant? Do you remember him, Rei?"

"No, that's not it. I mean—"

"The police are outside, but Dr. Anderson advised against talking to them until you get further rest." The nurse glances from me to Asher. "I can call them in."

"It's better if she rests first. I'm sure you understand with how much she's been through." He offers a million-dollar smile that might or might not end up being a serial killer's charming grin while he picks up his victims.

Even as I fight to get out from under his hold, I can't deny how fatally attractive he is.

Is it…lust?

That's the only reason I would be engaged to someone like him.

Well, shit. That's even worse than losing my memories. Please tell me I'm not vain enough to glue myself to such an asshole just because of lust.

"You're right." The nurse falls into his scheme so easily, so readily. It would be ironic if I weren't melting on the inside.

How can she not see his deception? His blatant lies?

She pats my hand on her way out. "The meds will take effect soon."

"N-no—" My words are cut off when he muffles my mouth with his hand.

The door hisses open then closed after the nurse. I mumble, feeling my breath being cut off more with every second.

My lungs burn and my eyes well with tears at the lack of air.

I can't breathe.

Shit. I can't breathe.

My nails dig into his arm even with the crippling

pain at my shoulder. Instead of letting me go, he watches my struggle with a curious glint, as if he wants to watch how I die. How I spit my last breath.

He's going to kill me, isn't he?

I came back to life just to die all over again.

My self-preservation instinct kicks in. I can't die. My nails dig into his hard skin with all the energy I have, scratching and clawing.

He doesn't budge.

If anything, his smirk widens, as if this is a circus and I'm his favorite act.

When I think I'm about to die, he removes his hand with ease. I suck in sharp breaths, choking on air.

Something soulless and dark creeps into his eyes, turning them almost black. "You think you can fight me?"

He strokes my hair behind my ear. The gesture is so gentle my breath catches. The way he flips between softness and cruelty is giving me whiplash.

All this is an act. Those dark eyes aren't capable of kindness. It's either a show or some fucked-up reverse psychology.

"You think anyone can save you from me?" He laughs, the sound hollow and deranged. "You're mine to screw and destroy, my ugly monster. It's time to get used to that."

I open my mouth to protest.

He shoves his finger against my lips, cutting off my words. "Shut it. You don't get to talk. You only get to listen."

The pulse in his forefinger beats against my mouth —constant, calm, and…cold.

Is it even possible for a pulse to feel this cold?

My lips are dry and sore, so I don't attempt to bite him like my brain is telling me to. If I clamp my teeth around his finger, he might seek revenge in a more brutal way.

My body is already too weak, bursts of pain starting at my nape and shoulders and extending to my limbs. I just need him gone until I'm strong enough to face him.

What's the best way to push him away without force?

Think. Think.

I meet his somber eyes and the harsh gleam shining in that green. It's such a shame an asshole like him has such a beautiful color.

I could forget my dignity and go with the pleading route, but I doubt it'd work on him.

There's so much unhinged hatred radiating off him.

So much…destruction.

I choose an entirely different route.

Darting my tongue out, I feel around his finger, licking the skin slowly.

Surprise registers in his eyes before his lids quickly lower halfway.

Yes. He can hide it all he likes, but I surprised him. People are easier to handle when they're taken off guard.

Especially demons like Asher. He seems to be the type who has everything under control, and I bet on that when I started licking his skin.

I meet his punishing gaze with my defiant one.

You won't get to me. Not now. Not ever.

His upper lip twitches as if he heard my internal challenge and accepted it.

He thrusts his finger inside my mouth, coiling it against my tongue. I gasp, but the sound is muted by his forceful shove.

His shoulders broaden even more and he appears like the Grim Reaper out to harvest lives—starting with mine.

My teeth graze his skin, and I pause, contemplating my next move.

"Bite and I'll hurt you back," he says, as if hearing my thoughts.

I glare up at him but continue.

The harder he glides his finger against my tongue,

the faster I lick, lapping against his single digit.

The more diligent I become, the more furious his eyes turn. No idea if it's rage or lust or both.

A flash of heat coils down my spine the more I suck him, but I don't stop. If I keep that look in his eyes, he'll leave me in peace.

My mouth opens farther as I take more of his forefinger inside. I don't even know what I'm doing, but I feel something seeping out of him and rushing to me.

A sense of power.

A shift in dynamics.

His mask is slipping and a demented gleam shines in his eyes.

I can keep on disarming him, and soon, he won't only leave me be, he might as well disappear from my life and—

He pulls his finger back as suddenly as he shoved it inside, and I release it with a pop.

His face returns to the calm façade, the impenetrable façade.

My breathing comes out harsh and irregular as I try to regain control over my senses.

Exhaustion rears on my nerve endings and my lids slowly flutter closed. Must be the meds. Good—something to take away the pain.

The bed shifts as Asher stands up, staring down at me with malice and...something else.

Maybe it's that something else, or maybe it's the fact I have no one here except for him. I just don't want to be alone.

The company of a monster is better than no company.

In the haziness of sleep, I murmur, "Don't...leave."

"You owe me. I'm not leaving anymore."

WHEN I WAKE up the next day, a small part of me hopes whatever happened yesterday was a nasty nightmare.

I'm not in the hospital. I didn't lose my memories. I don't have a fiancé who calls me a monster.

The white walls surrounding me and the scent of bleach negate the first option.

My heartbeat picks up when I search my surroundings for those sinister, terrifying eyes. My entire body kicks into gear, tightening and shuddering for a fight.

He's not here.

I release a breath. Maybe that part was indeed a nightmare.

"Reina?"

My muscles lock as I turn to my side. Pain explodes

in the back of my head and I wince. It's like a dull ache gripping my entire system.

"Take it easy, Rei." An older man's face comes into view as he helps me into a comfortable sitting position.

He's wearing a dark brown, Italian-cut suit. His short, dark hair is styled to perfection and his sharp green eyes look so much like…Asher.

"You're Asher's father?"

"You remember me." He smiles, and it reaches his eyes. "I was worried when the doctors mentioned amnesia."

"I still don't remember. You just look so much like him."

"I see." He unbuttons his jacket and sits down on the stool beside me. "I'm Alexander Carson, Asher's father and your guardian of sorts."

"My guardian? Aren't I twenty-one?"

"Almost twenty-one, yes. I was your legal guardian until you turned eighteen, and since you continued to study in Blackwood, I remain your next of kin."

Oh. Okay.

"Then that should mean Asher and I aren't engaged." I couldn't hold in the smile in my voice even if I tried.

It *was* a nightmare.

"Yes, you are, Rei."

My good mood falls like an atomic bomb. "I can't be engaged to my foster brother."

He smiles in a reassuring kind of way, like the nurse. "I became your legal guardian your senior year of high school, but you and Asher were engaged long before that. Besides, you never really lived together. Asher has been studying at Oxford for the past three years."

Oxford. That's in England. Phew. So he'll go back there and leave me here in peace.

Problem solved.

I focus back on Asher's father with newfound interest. Unlike Asher's, his eyes are a lighter green with a meaner shape. His lips are thinner, too. It's a profile of a man in power, I don't know how I know it, but I do.

"You said you became my legal guardian my senior year?"

He passes me a glass of water, and I drink even though I'm not thirsty. "Correct."

"W-what happened to my parents?" My heartbeat skyrockets and I grip the glass tight as I wait for his reply. Something tells me I won't like it.

A sheen of sadness covers his features. "Your mother died during childbirth and you lost your father in an accident. Gareth was my best friend and partner. He named me as your guardian in his will."

Oh.

Pressure builds behind my eyes and a strange sense of grief hits me. It's not only because of my parents' deaths, but also because I don't remember any of it.

How could I forget my own parents?

No.

I *have* parents. Deep down, I think I do have parents somewhere.

Alexander pats my hand with deep sympathy that touches my heart. His attitude is a million times different from that of his devil son. If it weren't for the uncanny physical resemblance, I would've never linked the two together.

"One step at a time, Rei." He offers a reassuring look. "We've got this."

A wave of tears assaults me, welling in my eyes.

Those are the words I've yearned to hear the most since I woke up with my head wiped clean. I wanted someone to console me and tell me everything will be okay. Instead, I had my freaking fiancé calling me a monster and threaten to break me.

I swallow back the need to cry. "Thank you, Mr. Carson."

"It's Uncle Alex to you, or just Alex if you don't feel the familiarity yet." He pats my hand once more before standing. "You should freshen up. The police are here for you. Remember, don't answer anything you don't feel like answering. I've already informed them about your memory loss. They're well aware your testimony won't be much, but they'll try to push anyway."

I nod slowly.

The nurse from yesterday comes inside, wearing a serene, welcoming expression.

I can't help searching behind her, expecting the nightmare from yesterday to show up with the intention of harvesting my soul.

Oxford, remember? Our engagement can't even be real if we've lived apart for more than three years. Long-distance relationships aren't known to work—not that I had any relationship with that psycho.

The nurse, Erika, exchanges some pleasantries with me as she helps me into a wheelchair.

Aside from the pain at the back of my head and my shoulders, my arms are sore and my legs are covered in blue and green bruises as if someone beat me up with the intention of killing me. I can't stand up on my right leg; the doctor mentioned something about a bad sprain.

After Erika helps me use the toilet, I place both arms on the sink as support and stand up. Pain snaps to my nape and my one good, unsteady leg. I bite my lower lip and remain still, panting, trying to let the agony pass.

I freeze as I stare ahead.

A galaxy of green, blue, and purple bruises cover my cheek, starting near my eye and spanning down to the hollow of my neck.

Still, the face that greets me in the mirror is familiar.

Way too familiar.

I have a slim, tall body like a model. My round breasts are high and perky, and I appear fit as if I work out for a living.

My exotic, blue eyes are so huge it's scary with all the bruises surrounding them. It's almost as if whoever beat me was seconds away from clawing my eyes out.

A shiver dances down my spine at the thought.

What could I have done to elicit such strong hatred? Or was I simply a victim of being in the wrong place at the wrong time?

My strawberry blonde hair reaches my shoulders in waves. Light blondish highlights add a beautiful hue at the tips. It's greasy and could use a wash, though.

What type of dye did I use to achieve this color?

I'm a natural, bitch.

The voice in the back of my head startles me.

Okay, natural it is.

For long seconds, I continue watching my image in the mirror. If I recognize that face as my own, how come I don't remember anything about myself? How come I don't even remember why my face looks like it's just come out of a battlefield?

My head hurts just thinking about it, so I let Erika wheel me back to the room.

"Do you feel better today?" she asks.

"I'm good, thanks." Now that Asher the jerk isn't here, I feel a whole lot better.

The smile she offers me is motherly and warm. "Asher spent the entire night with you and didn't leave until your guardian came. How sweet is that?"

Not at all.

I'm seriously contemplating asking if they have surveillance cameras so I can see if he did something to me in my sleep.

Paranoid much? Probably, but I don't trust that asshole. Not at all.

As soon as we're in the room, we're greeted by two police officers and an older man wearing a hat.

Alexander takes me from Erika with a polite nod. He maneuvers my chair so he's behind me and I'm facing the officers.

"Reina," he says, "This is Detective Daniels."

The detective appears to be in his mid-forties with a strong bone structure and sharp brown eyes that have been watching me closely since I came in.

He offers his hand, and I take it. "I'm sorry for what happened to you, Miss Ellis."

"Thank you."

He doesn't sit down as he retrieves his notepad. "Do you recall where you were the night between last Friday and Saturday?"

I try to concentrate, but I find a blank page. Sighing, I shake my head.

"We already asked your friends and classmates. You were last seen at the Black Devils' Friday night game."

"Black Devils?" I look between him and Alexander.

The latter smiles. "Black Devils is the name of your college's football team. You're the captain of the cheerleading squad."

Oh. Okay. I'm the captain of some devil cheerleaders. That totally makes sense.

No wonder I've been beaten up.

Also, cheerleading in college? How cliché can my life get? Kill me now, please.

"Do you remember who assaulted you, Miss Ellis?" Detective Daniels asks.

"No. I…I remember nothing prior to waking up in the hospital."

"Think carefully." The detective leans closer until his face is a few inches away from mine. "Your testimony could help solve an important case that occurred at the same time as your assault."

"Detective." Alexander's voice hardens with a warning. "I told you Reina is suffering from retrograde amnesia. Don't push her."

"No." I stop Alexander with a hand on his arm. "I want to help. What happened that night, detective?"

He narrows his eyes the same way Asher did when he seemed to not believe me. It's like they think I'm building a persona or something.

"There was a fire in a cottage not far from where you were found. We retrieved ashes of human remains that were scattered all over the place. We're investigating a homicide, Miss Ellis. Do you remember anything about what happened? Maybe you were there?"

My heart roars so loud as I focus on his words.

Human remains.

A homicide.

Oh, God.

"I-I don't know." Tears well in my eyes. "I really don't—"

"Don't answer that, Reina." Alexander cuts off my jumbled words.

Detective Daniels pulls out a plastic bag containing a dainty bracelet. Then he retrieves a picture of me wearing a black and white cheerleading outfit with the same bracelet around my wrist. "We found this bracelet inside the burnt cottage, and we believe you do know something."

"I…I don't." Or at least I don't remember.

"That's only circumstantial evidence, detective. No judge will give you a warrant for that." Alexander speaks with a coolness that intimidates me even though he's not addressing me. "Return with more concrete evidence. Until then, you will not harass my client or I'll file a restraining order."

Client?

"Very well." The detective stands up, looking at me with a hardened expression. "We'll be seeing each other again, Miss Ellis."

He waves the bracelet in front of my face, and something inside me snaps.

That's mine. He has no right to take what's mine.

Before I can voice my thoughts, the detective saunters out of the room with the officers following close behind him.

"Never mind him, Reina." Alexander faces me. "You're safe."

"He… Does he suspect me of murder?"

"He only has circumstantial evidence, and it means nothing." He clutches my shoulder. "My entire firm will defend you until the last breath we have. Don't worry about it."

A firm.

His confidant aura and legal talk make sense. He's a lawyer and owns a firm. That explains the expensive-looking hospital.

He said he'll defend me, but does it really matter if I'm an actual suspect and had a hand in hurting someone?

Dr. Anderson comes in with some interns, saying he needs to do a few more tests before my discharge.

Alexander spends most of the time talking on the phone about clients and lawsuits.

We stay a few more hours in the hospital, where I go through multiple tests and cognitive activities. While we wait for the results, Erika helps me shower and put on new clothes Alexander brought.

Seeming satisfied with my results, Dr. Anderson signs my discharge papers.

Alexander wheels my chair out toward a black, shiny Mercedes in front of which a driver wearing a sharp suit holds the door open.

A German car and a driver—of course. I should've pieced it all together.

Something glints in the distance as we stop near the door. I shield my eyes with the back of my hand. A slender figure stands near the corner, wearing a black hoodie and holding something shiny. I could almost swear the glint is directed at me. I squint to get a better view. The figure and the glint disappear altogether.

I crane my head, searching the corner.

Nothing.

It's like they were never there.

Please tell me that wasn't a play of my imagination.

"What is it, Reina?" Alexander follows my field of vision.

"N-nothing." My brain is probably still trying to keep up with the outside world.

Alexander and the driver help me into the backseat. The wheelchair goes in the trunk. Then we hit the road.

My 'guardian' busies himself with his phone as I watch the city's tall buildings through the half-lowered window. The colors are so vibrant and... alive. So why do I feel anything but?

Chaos and the unknown gnaw at my chest like the prickling of tiny needles.

I lean over, letting the wind blow my hair back. It would've felt nice under different circumstances.

I close the window and slowly face Alexander. "Where are we going?"

He lifts his head from his phone. "Since you're still

weak, you should move back in with me until you're stronger."

"Where did I used to live?"

"In an apartment close to the center of town." He pauses. "There's been a break-in during your stay in the hospital."

"A b-break-in? Why?"

"We don't know. Nothing was stolen."

My brows furrow. "How come the detective didn't mention that? It could be motive, right?"

"I didn't report it." His face is hard. "You don't want the police to sniff around you, Reina."

"But why? Aren't I the victim in this?"

"You are, but you're also Gareth Ellis' only heir. Our families don't like attention from anyone, police included."

There's something he's not telling me, but what?

His face breaks into a smile and I recognize that he shut off the subject altogether. "My house is your house. And don't worry, Blackwood College isn't far."

"Okay." I would rather stay with someone who clearly cares about my well-being than being alone anyway.

"Are you ready to go home, Reina?"

Does it matter when I don't even know where my home is?

CHAPTER 6 - REINA

HOME IS A MANSION.

The house is three stories and so big I don't see the end of it. It's even located on the outskirts of town, which means Alexander is a private man.

The entire front of the house is made of glass. The whole scene seems more like a monumental museum than a place where people live.

A circular garden surrounds the front of the house with trees cut into geometrical shapes. Beds of colorful tulips and roses decorate the space between trees.

A kidney-shaped pool sits in the distance. A low, thumping of music comes from that direction.

Alexander pushes my wheelchair, telling me about the house, how I brought it to life when I used to live here and how he left my room unchanged. He shows me the vast grassy area where I used to practice my moves for the cheerleading squad.

Apparently, I've been a cheerleader since high school. Even though I'm studying human sciences at Blackwood, I still cheer for the team.

Seriously, why the hell would I continue doing that stuff three years after high school?

The more I learn about myself, the clearer the picture becomes.

My entire life is like a jigsaw of plastic pieces.

I'm rich—well, Alexander is. My father could've been rich too since he was best friends with him.

"What did my father do?" I ask Alexander.

"Gareth was a real estate mogul." His tone is sad, and it affects me, too.

"So he was rich?"

"Rich?" He laughs with no humor. "He was a tycoon, Rei. He owned half of Blackwood, and now you do, of course."

I couldn't care less whether I'm rich or not, but for some reason, I'm glad I have some sort of independence. I'd hate to think Alex took me in as a type of charity case.

"Your father was…" He trails off as if weighing his words. "He had some connection to a bad crowd, so if you remember anything, tell me first."

My spine jerks upright as I slowly turn around in my chair. Alex stands there with a neutral expression.

"What type of bad crowd?"

"It's better if you don't know."

"I knew before I lost my memories, right?"

"Not exactly."

"Alex." My tone turns pleading. "Have you seen my face? Someone wanted me dead. If there's a threat to my life, I have the right to know."

He halts in front of majestic double doors with a black and white marble pattern, and pinches the bridge of his nose. "Gareth did business with the mafia. Italian, Russian. You name it."

"T-the mafia?"

"Correct. I have my suspicions considering your assault."

"You think they did this to me? Dad's enemies?"

He stands in front of me, sparing me the pain of leaning back. My neck muscles sag in relief when I return at a normal angle.

"They weren't your dad's enemies, that's why it's weird they're coming after you, let alone three years after his death." He crouches in front of me. "I'm your lawyer, Reina. If there's anything I need to know, tell me."

"I-I don't know." My tongue feels heavy in my

mouth. "Why are you so sure it's the mafia? Can't it be someone else?"

"This has their fingerprints all over it. The assault, the break-in, and the black van that was camped near the hospital as soon as you were admitted."

That's bad. Super bad. "Does this mean I'm still in danger?"

"They disappeared, but they can always return."

"The police?"

He scoffs. "They're useless and they think Gareth's business is still tied to the mob. They're after you, not with you, Reina. You need to understand that."

"I do."

"I need to know what we're dealing with. If you remember anything, I have to be the first to know, okay?"

I nod slowly.

Alex nods back and rises to his feet, then wheels me inside. My heartbeat hammers at the load of information I just learned. The mafia. Why the hell would my father get involved with something so dangerous and where do I fit in the entire picture?

A plump woman with bright blonde hair quickens her footsteps toward us. She stops and wipes her hands on her apron, gaze kind but distant.

"Welcome back, Miss Reina. I hope you're feeling better." She speaks with a slight Southern accent.

I stare at Alex, silently asking who she is.

"This is Elizabeth," he says. "She takes care of the house."

"So it's true." The corners of her eyes pull downward. "You remember nothing."

I nod slowly, feeling awful that I've completely wiped her—and everyone else—from my memory.

"It's okay, darlin'." She takes my wheelchair from Alex's hands.

He places his phone to his ear as he takes the stairs to the left. "Elizabeth will take good care of you. Let me know if you need anything, Reina."

He disappears before I can say anything.

"He's a busy man, isn't he?" I ask Elizabeth.

"I'm surprised he took the time to bring you home from the hospital—" She cuts herself off and quickly follows with, "Not that he wasn't worried about you. He was, but…well—"

"His work comes first." I finish for her.

"Well, yes."

I kind of figured that out with the amount of time he spent on the phone the whole way here.

"He does care, though," she murmurs, as if speaking to herself.

Once we reach the stairs, I place my hands on the armrests of the chair and attempt to stand up. Soreness erupts throughout my muscles.

"It's okay." Elizabeth tries to keep me down. "I'll call Jason to come and help carry you up."

"No need." I stand, using the railing for balance. Something tells me I hate imposing on people or asking them for something I can do on my own.

The sound of the music continues thumping from outside.

"On second thought." I sit back down and try to maneuver the chair without triggering the pain in my shoulders.

"You okay there, darlin'?" Elizabeth keeps me in place, stopping me from falling sideways.

"Yeah. I want to see what's going on outside."

"Well...umm..." Her gaze darts back and forth.

"What is it?"

"It's better you don't."

"What do you mean? Who's out there?"

"Your college friends."

I smile. "One more reason to meet them."

Maybe like Dr. Anderson said, seeing familiar faces will finally shake me out of this zombie trance and give me something to look forward to.

Like regaining my memories.

"Right." She pauses, glancing sideways as if trying to find a way out—of what, I don't know. "Maybe it's because you don't remember that you don't care, but the old Reina would never let others see her this way."

I glance down at myself and the simple denim dress the nurse helped me put on at the hospital. Before we left, Erika helped me wash and dry my hair. It's neatly tucked into a ponytail, and I look presentable enough. There shouldn't be a reason why Elizabeth would think otherwise.

"What way?" I ask.

She motions at my face. "All bruised and not in top shape."

"Don't tell me I used to get done up to meet my friends?"

"Done up?" She laughs in a heartfelt way. "You never stepped outside unless you looked like a goddess."

Okay, that's even more superficial than anything I've heard about my life thus far. Why would I care so much about my appearance when, according to the picture the detective showed me, I'm naturally pretty?

It's not like I'm a model or something.

An urge pushes me to go see what's going on out there, but what Elizabeth just told me stops me in place.

I can't go against what the old me used to do just because I want to.

I must've had a reason for acting the way I did.

Deep down, I refuse to believe I'm that vain or plastic or another stereotypical cheerleader.

Unless I figure out my reasons for having them in the first place, I can't break any patterns. I can't ruin my life just because I lost my memories.

Besides, as Dr. Anderson said, all of this is temporary. I'll remember everything sooner rather than later.

Right?

A commotion comes from a huge double door to our right. Male and female voices and laughter filter in all at once.

"We can hide in the kitchen," Elizabeth whispers, turning my chair.

I clutch her hand, stopping her. I might not want to ruin Old Reina's lifestyle, but I'm not running away in what's supposed to be my home.

Sure, I don't remember it, but it still counts as my home.

My confidence crumbles the moment I make eye contact with the person I never wanted to see again.

Asher.

Isn't he supposed to be at Oxford? Alex said he studied in England, didn't he?

He *should* be in England.

He laughs along at something someone said at his side, but his entire focus is on me.

Like a hunter.

The air ripples with tension and dark intentions. It licks at my skin like rusty knives.

Dark aviators sit on his straight, arrogant nose, so I can't see his eyes, and it pisses me off.

I can't get a read on him, and I feel like I always need to predict his moves.

He's wearing white shorts and a black T-shirt that tightens around his cut abdomen and sculpted biceps.

Since I'm sitting, he appears taller than I initially predicted at the hospital. If anything, the lines of his face are sharper and harder, too.

Shouldn't assholes be less handsome?

"Oh my Gosh, Reina. Are you okay?" A squeaky feminine voice snatches my attention.

She's a petite girl with curves highlighted by her bikini top and denim shorts that reveal the crack of her ass. Her long blonde hair falls down her back, the same color as mine—only hers doesn't appear natural.

Her upper body leans into Asher's side as if she's hugging him by the waist. When she notices me watching her movement, she pulls back a little with 'oops' written all over her face.

I narrow my eyes but quickly seal that reaction away. For some reason, I don't think Old Reina showed emotions. If she didn't show her makeup-free face, she likely didn't reveal anything else.

"And you are?" I ask in a cool tone.

"Brianna. You call me Bree—we're, like, best friends!" she squeals, clutching my hands in hers.

I wince as pain shoots up my arm and to my sore shoulders.

She pulls her hand back quickly, and the pain doubles as my arms fall to my lap. "Oops, sorry. I guess what Asher said is true—you don't remember." She throws him a look over her shoulder. "You didn't tell us it was this bad."

Did he have to? If her so-called *best friend* was in an accident and was admitted to the hospital for a week, shouldn't she have visited? Or at least not partied at the pool with said friend's freaking fiancé?

And why the hell is that fiancé still here anyway?

A tall shirtless man pushes past her and crouches in front of me. He sports a beautiful tan that complements his dark brown eyes. He narrows them on me as if trying to read something in my face. "You really remember nothing?"

"Of course she doesn't." Another blond man in a polo shirt, khaki shorts, and mirror sunglasses stands beside Asher. "Or else she wouldn't look like a zombie in front of us."

Elizabeth leans over to whisper in my ear. "The polo guy is Sebastian. The one kneeling is Owen. Both are Asher's friends and play for the Black Devils."

I nod, trying to associate the names to the faces. It's not working so well in my head.

"He's right." Bree's brows furrow, but I can't help detecting how fake her concern is. "The girls and boys are right outside. You don't want them to see you this way, Rei."

"Maybe she does." Asher finally speaks after watching from afar like a creep.

I don't actually believe whatever engagement we have is genuine, so I don't care that he didn't come to the hospital with Alex. The least he could do, however, is not throw a pool party while I struggle to move.

I throw him a glare before I address Bree. "I just got home from the hospital. I'd rather get some sleep."

"Yeah, right. Sure." She pats my hand with mock sympathy. "Don't worry about the squad. I'm holding down the fort just fine."

Uh-huh. Why do I feel like that was supposed to be a jab toward me?

"Sure," I say anyway.

"Wait." The one named Owen—who's still kneeling

in front of me—cuts in. "You really remember nothing?"

I nod.

"How about the blowjob you promised me after the last game?"

My eyes snap to Asher. He remains completely still, as if his friend didn't just suggest I give him a blowjob.

His blank face is a mystery on its own. I don't know if it's a lack of reaction or a completely different way of showing it.

Meeting Owen's gaze, I say, "What do I get out of that promise?"

He pauses, taken aback. "What?"

"I wouldn't promise to blow you if I wasn't going to get something out of it."

Asher smirks while Sebastian laughs.

"Well, fuck, girl." Owen stands up. "You look like a zombie but your tongue hasn't changed."

I raise an eyebrow. "Should it?"

"Maybe."

"Or maybe not," I counter.

Asher moves in my peripheral vision and I could almost swear he was about to say something, but he stops.

Another man comes inside from where Elizabeth walked in earlier. He's tall with mocha skin and curly black hair. He smiles, and unlike any of the four surrounding me, it reaches his eyes. I mirror it, my heart feeling light. For some reason, I feel like I know him.

Really know him.

"Jason," Elizabeth says with glee. "You've come just in time."

"How you doin', Reina?" He stops beside me. "So sorry I couldn't visit. Mom didn't tell me."

Elizabeth laughs awkwardly. "He was at camp. You know, it's the beginning of the season, Miss Reina."

"It's okay." I smile up at both of them. "I'm alive, after all."

"And apparently with no memories." Asher's biting tone comes from my side.

Apparently with no memories.

What is that supposed to mean?

I ignore him and focus on Jason's kind expression.

"Well, what are you doin'?" Elizabeth ushers him. "Help me get Miss Reina upstairs."

He moves, but Asher steps in front of him. "I'll do it."

I lift a hand. "I want Jason to do it."

Asher freezes, and although I can't see his eyes, the tightening of his jaw is enough to relay his displeasure.

Screw him.

He obviously doesn't care about me. He made it clear he wants to harm me. If he thinks I'll just sit here and watch, he has another thing coming.

Owen elbows Sebastian, and the latter remains frozen in place.

Bree laughs in a long, squeaky shrill. "Let the help do it, Asher. It's not worth your time."

"Yes." Elizabeth laughs, and it's obvious she's trying to make up for the awkward tension in the air. "Jason can do it."

"He's not *the help*," I hiss at Bree. "When you're at my house, you respect everyone in it."

Silence fills the hall. Everyone watches me closely, as if I've grown two heads. What? Isn't that the right thing to say?

Bree releases an awkward laugh before she whispers, "Come on, Rei. You call him the help yourself."

I…I do?

My fingers turn clammy as my hands strangle each other. No. She's lying. I'm not snobbish or cruel enough to call him that.

"I'm fine to do it." Jason advances forward.

Asher blocks his way. They're similar build-wise, but Asher is taller so he blocks Jason's expression.

He yanks me from my chair so fast, pain explodes all over my limbs.

My arms go around his neck for balance as my body fits into his arms easily. An unwelcome shiver dances down my spine. "Ever heard of being gentle?"

"Do you deserve gentle?" His hot breath forms goosebumps on the shell of my ear as he murmurs, "Monster?"

"Put me down," I hiss.

"Only if it's to throw you in hell, but it's too early for that."

I try to escape his brutal hold. One of his arms is around my midsection like a vise, and the other squeezes the bruise on my thigh.

Oh, God. That hurts like a bitch.

"Stay. Fucking. Still." He enunciates every word with a cold edge.

And then he ignores everyone and takes me up the stairs.

CHAPTER 7 - REINA

"LET ME GO!" I hit his chest; it's hard and stone-like. All I manage to do is hurt my fist.

His wide strides cut through the long hallway. Stainless marble and crystal chandeliers decorate the ceiling above us.

After a few moments of useless struggle, I realize I'll only hurt myself. I huff and opt to choose my battles.

Still, I glare at Asher, letting him know my opinion of what he's doing. Since he's wearing the damned sunglasses, I don't get to see his expression.

I pluck them away.

It's his turn to throw a quizzical glance in my direction.

"What? We're indoors. Why the hell are you wearing shades?"

He narrows his eyes the slightest bit but says nothing.

I look behind me, but no one followed us, not even Elizabeth. Maybe they all idolize him like the nurse in the hospital did.

That thought makes me pause.

He gave an extremely positive image at the hospital, and even earlier, he acted like some sort of a doting asshole by offering to carry me.

Am I really the only one who knows how screwed up in the head he is?

"Where's your engagement ring?" he asks.

"An engagement ring?"

"You heard me, where is it?"

"I…don't know." And I really don't. Now that I think about it, I should have one but I don't.

Asher says nothing as we go into a large bedroom—scratch that, a princess bedroom. There's a queen-sized bed with pink and beige sheets and a desk, on top of which sit countless pictures of me in a cheerleading outfit. Said outfit is hanging on the door of an open walk-in closet.

No kidding—it's a whole walk-in. There are a few plaid skirts, white button-downs, and black jackets, on which there's a golden symbol. My uniform from high school, I assume.

Private school. Of course I went to a private school. It fits the whole snobbish image.

Reina Ellis.

Captain of the cheerleading squad.

Doesn't go out without makeup.

Heir to Daddy's fortune.

And engaged to a jerk who couldn't care less about me.

I really want to sit down with Old Reina and discuss her options. Surely she could've done better.

And yes, I'm judging myself. It's my only option to vent.

"Let me go, Asher," I spit out.

He throws me on the bed. I groan as my bruised hipbone hits the mattress.

What the hell? That *hurts*.

When I glare up at him, he gives me an indecipherable expression and places both his hands in his pockets. "You said to let you go."

"Why do you hate me so much?" *If you do, why the hell are you engaged to me?*

"Might have to do with how much of a bitch you are."

"Oh, I'm sorry." I smile. "Did I steal your title, asshole?"

He pauses, head tilting to the side. "What did you just call me?"

"A-S-S-H-O-L-E." I continue smiling, taunting him. "Do you want me to spell it for you again—"

My words cut off when he's at my face, kneeling on the bed in front of me. His hand wraps around my throat like a shackle. He's not squeezing, but the firm grip is enough to restrict my air supply and my thoughts.

A frightening chill forms goosebumps along my skin as I stare at his darkened, merciless eyes.

The sense of bravery I gained a few seconds ago evaporates into thin air. My shoulder blades snap together as if telling me I should be scared.

This is a scary person.

He's fucking terrifying.

The need to run away from him hits me again, clawing under my skin and pumping in my blood.

"You seem to be taking your amnesia game way too seriously, so let me remind you of how it goes." His thumb rubs my jaw like a lover's caress when in fact it's a Grim Reaper's kiss.

It's cold.

Everything about him is freezing.

My pulse roars in my ears like a distant thunderstorm.

He's invading my space like a natural disaster, impossible to stop or prevent.

Still, I manage to choke words out. "You think this is a game? What type of person pretends to have lost their memories?"

"The type who doesn't want people to know what they've done."

"What I've done?"

"Shhh. Don't talk." He presses his thumb to my lips, and I can't help the pulses taking flight under my skin. "When I speak, you listen."

Despite the shivers of fear bursting through my system, my temper flares. Who the hell does this asshole think he is?

It takes effort, but I tell him point-blank, "You're not my keeper, Ash."

He pauses, and his hold loosens on my throat a little as if I've caught him off guard. The lapse lasts for a fraction of a second before his mask is strapped back on his face and his clutch tightens.

"It's Asher. You don't call me that. *Ever.*"

I want to taunt him, but that would be stupid with his hand around my throat this way. I'm seriously starting to think he's a psycho, and psychos don't think twice before suffocating their victims.

Or snapping their necks.

"Shouldn't you be in England?" My vocal cords strain with the effort it takes to say the words. "Alex said you study at Oxford."

He raises an eyebrow. "Not anymore."

"Not anymore?" What the hell is that supposed to mean? I was only enduring his jerk ways because he's supposed to fly to another continent.

As if reading my mind, his lips twitch in a smirk as he strokes my jaw with his lean thumb. "I can't leave my fiancée alone, now can I?"

Screw him to the darkest pits of hell.

We both know that's not the case. He's only staying here to torment me and turn my life into a nightmare.

More than he already is.

"Don't take the help's side over mine." All his good —or fake—mood disappears, replaced by a cold, hard-ened expression. "Is that understood?"

I remain motionless, not uttering a word. If I do, I'll yell profanities, and then he'll really choke me to death.

It's crazy how much his energy seeps under my skin even when I try to chase it away.

It's like hypnotism.

That's it—I'm being hypnotized.

He squeezes his thumb against the hollow of my throat. "I said, is that fucking understood?"

"Whatever you say, Ash." I try to keep the tremors and fear out of my voice by inserting as much sarcasm as I can.

Big mistake.

His hand turns to steel as he squeezes hard. My eyes bulge as my small air supply vanishes.

I claw at his hand, scratching the skin. Just like in the hospital, he doesn't budge.

The damn psycho is out for my life.

"What was that?" he asks, slightly loosening his hold.

"Asher! Asher!"

He removes his hand, but he doesn't back off.

I cough, massaging my assaulted throat. "Jeez. It's just a name."

He stares at me for a second too long, as if he's trying to figure out how to deal with me and…failing.

"Cut the crap. Where were you going that night?" he asks in a calm tone, as if he didn't just attempt to end my life.

"Ever heard of amnesia? It means I don't remember." I point at my head. "I don't even know why the hell I'm with someone like you."

"You're not *with* me."

Both his hands grip my bare thighs and pull me forward so my legs are on either side of his kneeling position. I yelp then gasp when his hands trail up until they reach the middle of my thighs. I try to escape, but he digs his fingers into my bruises, caging me against him.

"I *own* you. Every single part of you. You might have tried to escape, but that won't happen again. I don't know what kind of game you're playing this time, but I'll figure it out and you'll lose like you do every fucking time."

"I tried to escape?" I ask. "Why?"

From what? Or rather, who? Does it have something to do with Dad's mafia friends or with Asher or what exactly?

So many questions and no answer whatsoever.

"That's what I'm going to find out." He keeps a hand on my thigh, and brings the other to my face, placing his thumb on my lips. It's still cold like it was at the hospital, but my nerves keep tingling at the sensation.

Asher's dark eyelashes flutter over his somber gaze like a cloak, impenetrable and harsh. "Open your mouth."

If he thinks he gets a repeat of what happened at the hospital, then he's sorely mistaken. I only did that because it was a ploy to have him lower down his guards. Now that he's demanding it means he's in control, and I don't play with an Asher in control. That'll only mean he'll devour me alive and leave nothing behind.

"No." I jut my chin. "I won't do—"

"Shhh. Don't talk. When I speak, you listen. When I order, you obey. Now, open that fucking mouth."

How can he sound so authoritative and controlling when he says that? Is that how he always talks?

The arrogant bastard.

His voice gains a lethal edge. "If you don't, I'll make you, and it'll fucking hurt."

As if proving a point, his thumb presses on a bruise on my thigh. I cry out as the agony shoots through me; hot and red. He keeps his thumb at my lower lip and doesn't take advantage of my mouth opening. The asshole isn't interested in that; he wants me to forfeit.

The pain slowly subsides and I go back to glare at him. He's playing dirty with my condition.

His thumb strokes around the bruise eliciting a burst of slight comfort, pain, and a promise for more. I have no doubt that he'll push if I encourage him. It's like he has no limits.

"That's nothing compared to what I can do to you,

Reina." His thumb freezes and I do, too. "Are you or are you not going to open that mouth?"

My lips part, slowly but surely. I don't have the strength to play at his level now. With my injuries and his volatile personality, this can end badly for me. I have enough self-preservation to pick my battles.

He thrusts his thumb between my lips, and it takes everything in me not to bite down.

"Suck."

It's one word. One single word but it's charged with so much intensity, it's almost a living, breathing being.

He raises one perfect, thick eyebrow. "Do I have to threaten you again?"

Glaring up at him, I suck on his thumb faster than I intend to. My teeth graze his skin and I freeze, thinking he'll rule it as if I were trying to bite him. When he continues watching me with half-lowered lids, I continue slower this time.

My cheeks heat and I curse myself for giving in this easily. Wait until I'm stronger, I'm going to clash with him headfirst.

"What to do?" He deadpans. "You have a new problem, Reina."

I peek up at him, stopping.

"Did I tell you to stop?" He cocks his head to the side.

Groaning, I continue sucking the digit and lapping on it with my tongue.

"Your new problem is that you're too expressive. You're losing your touch."

Why is being expressive a problem? I glare up at him so he knows exactly how I feel about him.

I don't know what he expected, but my reaction is probably not it. Asher narrows his eyes before he pulls his finger out of my mouth. "I'll find out about that night, and I'll make you fucking wish you never set foot in the forest."

"You're a psycho." I breathe out, my heart stammering.

It keeps beating and pulsing like crazy, as if it'll soon stop and is using up all of its energy.

Asher's lips pull up in a cruel smirk. "It takes one to know one, my ugly monster."

He keeps calling me that, and I'm starting to think I should embrace that side to fight this particular monster off.

THE REST of the week is filled with doctor's appointments and trying to figure out who the hell I am.

I still can't remember anything prior to waking up in the hospital, and Dr. Anderson's diagnosis remains the same: my memories will filter back with time. However, at the last appointment, I heard him tell Alex we should be preparing for the possibility of this becoming long term.

I should be ready to live with a wiped memory.

Thinking about it brings a taste of bitterness and nausea. I'm not ready to face that bleak reality.

Today, I decided to end the one-person pity party and go back to college.

This is my last year, and I shouldn't miss more classes.

I can walk with a brace on my right leg, and there's no point in roaming around an empty house. Alex is barely home, if ever. Elizabeth—whom I finally convinced to let me call her Izzy—is usually holed up in the kitchen making some of the most delicious food I've ever tasted.

Every time I eat her meals, I wonder why the hell I would have moved out.

She's been giving me funny stares whenever I ask for more or for food rich in calories. Apparently, I only ate salads before. That's such a blasphemous thing to do when Izzy's food is around.

To my dismay, the resident asshole Asher hasn't left. I've been praying every day that the next time I wake up, he'll be long gone to England.

Hasn't happened.

On top of that, he enrolled in Blackwood College. I don't know why the hell he would give up Oxford and return here.

It can't be just so he can ruin my life.

Scratch that—with someone like Asher, it's completely plausible.

I've been actively avoiding him, which isn't too hard. We don't eat together in this family. Alex is off to work first thing in the morning and returns late. Asher leaves early, too. I watch him from my window. He's usually wearing jeans and stylish sports T-shirts.

Every day, he stops in front of the house and glances up. Sometimes, I'd swear he was looking straight at me if I weren't sure the curtains camouflaged me. Those annoying aviators hide his expression, too, so I'm never sure what he's thinking about.

No idea why I always want to know what's going on in that screwed-up head.

Asher is an enigma in a way, but that's not all. He's an enigma who's after me. I've been watching him closely with Izzy and the rest of the staff, and he never shows them an ounce of what he shows me.

If anything, he laughs and smiles like the kindest son of a bitch in the world.

It aches, you know. Being hated by someone who doesn't hate anyone is a straight jab to my person.

What could I have done to warrant such treatment?

Some days, I curl into a ball and let a gloomy depression take me over. I let the unknown creep under my skin and whisper nasty things to my brain.

Well, not today.

I have to start somewhere to know what kind of person I am. And yes, I've been praying I'm not the type who dresses to impress or a vain cheerleading captain.

A truck comes down the driveway, heading toward the entrance.

My chance.

Due to the brace, I limp and move slowly, but I manage to intercept Jason's truck before it's out.

The sound of the brakes echoes in the air. He rolls his window down. "Jesus. Do you have a death wish?"

I open the passenger door, throw my bag in, and slide inside. "Not today, but a ride to college would be cool."

Even though the inside of the truck isn't fancy, it smells like mint and lemon, like summer.

I like that smell.

He looks me up and down like I'm a zombie apocalypse runaway. I mean I'm wearing a denim dress and some cute flats I found at the back of the walk-in. I even covered all the bruises with foundation. The only thing that stands out is the leg brace that stops right under my knee. I shouldn't look that much like a zombie.

Jason grips the steering wheel, continuing the up-and-down examination. His expression isn't exactly one of interest, more like...surprise. "You're going back to college?"

"Yup, and you're giving me a ride."

He laughs. "Yeah, not going to happen, princess."

"I knew it." I narrow my eyes on him.

He narrows his eyes back. "You knew what?"

"You've been avoiding me since I came here. You can't run away. Spill, Jason." I try not to sound offended. I actually thought he could be my only friend here—until he disappeared from my immediate vicinity.

His brows furrow. "There's nothing to spill."

"You mean to tell me you haven't been around this past week and you don't want to give me a ride because you're *not* avoiding me?"

"First of all, I go to a cheaper college on the other side of town. If I go to your elite Blackwood College, I'll be skinned alive by the Knights."

"The Knights?"

"I play as a quarterback for the Knights, and the Black Devils are our number one rival. We have rivals week in town."

Still not sure why that matters.

"Second of all, we don't mingle, princess." He leans over, watching his surroundings before he whispers like some spy. "At least not in public."

My eyes widen. That means we mingle in private.

I knew it! I could feel the connection with Jason without having to try hard.

"What did we do in private?" I whisper back, somehow feeling like we need to keep quiet.

Jason opens his mouth to speak but soon closes it when he stares ahead.

I follow his line of sight.

Something constrictive balls at the back of my throat and my palms turn sweaty, all cold and wrong.

Asher.

He steps out of the house, wearing dark jeans and a gray T-shirt. The clothes are nothing special, but on him, they appear elegant, majestic even.

His hair is styled back, but it still has that rugged look, as if he only half bothered with it. As usual, the aviators sit on his arrogant nose like they're a part of his face.

Why the hell would someone with such mesmerizing eyes hide them?

Not that I think his eyes are mesmerizing. They're *not*.

He heads for the Mustang parked out front—of course an asshole drives such a beautiful car. It's black, too, like his soul.

He stops in front of his ride, as if feeling my attention on him.

Oh, no. It's not good if I'm caught in that asshole's

orbit. He'll just suck the life out of me like in the last encounters we've had.

I perk up and whisper-yell at Jason. "Go."

"Does anyone even know you're going to school?"

"Alex does." I *think*. He was too preoccupied in his office when I kind of informed him last night. He could've nodded to me or to whoever was on the phone; I'll never know. "Go before he sees us," I urge Jason.

"You're supposed to go with him."

I lift my chin up. "I'm supposed to be with whoever the hell I please. Asher is not my keeper."

At that exact moment, Asher lifts his head, and his shade-covered eyes collide with mine.

I swear some sort of battle erupts whenever we're in the same place.

He says something. I don't hear him, but I see him mouth 'Stop' as Jason kicks the truck into gear.

As we pass Asher, I roll down the window and flip him off. He freezes, a hand lying inert by his side. I soak in his surprised expression as Jason and I laugh.

"I've got to admit, I'm loving the new you," Jason says.

"Why? What was the old me like?"

"Bitchy? Snobby? Silent, mostly."

Ouch.

"And you would've never flipped Asher Carson the bird."

I raise an imaginary cup. "To the new me, I guess."

From today onward, no one is telling me how to live my life.

BLACKWOOD IS KIND OF what I expected from an
elite college.

It's four stories high and has ancient, European-ish
architecture. Two huge towers stand tall on each end
like a pair of massive guards.

The parking lot is filled with expensive cars, mostly
German like Alex's.

Jason parks the truck outside the college. It's close
enough so I won't have to walk a long distance but far
enough so no one can see him—or us.

I retrieve my bag. "You sure you don't want to
come in?"

His laughter echoes with genuine amusement like I
just told the most entertaining joke of the century. "The

only time I walk into the Black Devil's compound is to whoop their asses on their own field."

I roll my eyes. "Cocky much?"

"We might not have a lot of things going on, but we have ball. No snobby rich boys will take our championship away."

I guess the rivalry between the Knights and the Black Devils is a real thing.

Still maneuvering my bag around my body, I open the door and slowly get my injured leg out.

"Do you want me to help?" Jason asks from beside me.

"Nope." I mimic his earlier tone. "I might not remember anything, but I know how to take care of myself."

He chuckles, the sound easy and cool on the ears.

I pause with my hand on the handle. "What were we exactly, Jason? You and I?"

His chuckle dies and silence hangs between us like a third presence for a moment too long. Finally, he sighs. "Friends."

"Let me guess. We were only friends when my other friends weren't around?"

"Something like that." He grins. "But hey, it worked just fine."

Well, not anymore.

The old Reina might have had her reason for hiding her friendship with Jason, but I can't possibly find an excuse for it. True, I agreed not to disrupt my life, but I won't stand still in front of stupid decisions—like hiding my friendship with Jason.

I'll fix that part on Old Reina's behalf.

It takes me several excruciating minutes to climb down from the truck. After I wave at Jason, he retreats and speeds in the opposite direction.

I watch him for a few seconds until he disappears around the corner.

Okay. I'm on my own now.

I mean, it shouldn't be a problem. After all, I studied at this college for three years. It can't possibly be that hard…right?

Even as I repeat the pep talk in my head, that gloomy cloud creeps into my brain, filling it with dark thoughts.

No one cares about you.

You're nothing.

Absolutely nothing.

I briefly close my eyes and try my hardest to push those damning thoughts away. They won't get the best of me.

Not today.

The moment I open my eyes, a black van retreats

slowly from around the corner. The windows are tinted black, and there's no way to see who's inside.

My shoulder blades stiffen, and my nails dig into my bag's strap. Are those the people Alex said watched me when I was admitted to the hospital?

The mafia.

How did they know where to find me? Did they follow us from home? Or maybe they were waiting for my return to college.

Sweat breaks out on my forehead as I remain frozen in place. I can't move or think or come up with an escape plan. Like a deer caught in headlights, I remain there, lips parted and eyes wild.

Don't stop. Don't look back. If you survive, I survive.

A familiar voice whispers in my head, and it's like a shot of adrenaline. Gripping my bag tight, I watch my surroundings looking for anyone. They can't hurt me when there are people around. The mob's rule is to leave no witnesses behind.

Wait. How do I know that?

Just when I'm about to make a run for the entrance —or rather, limp toward it—the van suddenly changes direction. The squeak of the tires echoes in the air as it speeds in the opposite way.

My shoulders droop, and I'm about to release a sigh

of relief when a familiar Mustang revs toward me at supersonic speed.

Oh, come on. Asher is the last thing I need for my screwed-up mood.

On second thought, did the van leave because he approached? Not that I'd ever be grateful to him or let him know that.

I ignore him and hobble to the entrance. Since it's still early in the morning, only a few people are scattered around. I wanted to come at this hour to take a small tour and get familiar with the building and the students.

Still, even with so few students, the back of my neck prickles with unwanted attention. I can't help feeling like a bug being examined underneath a microscope. Every move I make is measured by onlookers, and I have no clue who they are.

Maybe coming back all alone wasn't the best idea after all. As much as my initial interaction with Bree sucked, I should've probably tagged along with her on my first day here.

A strong arm circles my waist from behind. I'm about to struggle free when I feel the familiar coldness.

The freezing body.

Like ice in the middle of summer.

This close, the smell of his aftershave grips my

senses in a tight, merciless grip. Sandalwood and citrus. Rich but cold. He smells of fresh laundry right out of the dryer, but also of the darkness of the night.

He's an enigma that way, Asher.

He spins me around, and I wobble on my good foot so I don't make the other one worse.

He doesn't do it by force, though. I don't know why I expected him to kick me in the shin just to make my injury way more painful.

"What do you think you're doing?" He stares down at me with a cool expression. Those damn sunglasses block me from getting a read on him.

"What does it look like I'm doing? I'm going back to school."

"And you chose Jason for a ride." It's not a question; he's stating a fact, and he's intimidating me in such a subtle way, no passersby would detect it.

What kind of sorcery does he possess? Or maybe it's not sorcery at all. This is the face of someone who's in complete control of his emotions.

The type of demon who probably doesn't have them at all.

That could explain why he can switch his body language so fast.

But if he thinks I'll be his willing toy, he must really not know me at all. I might not have memories, but I know I'm not the type who lets others walk all over me.

I jut my chin out. "Jason and I are friends."

He clutches my arm, fingers digging into my tender skin, and pushes me toward the wall. I gasp as my back hits the solid stone. Both his hands slam on either side of my face as he leans so close I can see his darkened eyes through the aviators.

"You're not friends with Jason. You're not friends with anyone unless I say you are."

"Jeez, controlling much, Ash?"

He wraps his hand around my collarbone. It's firm, disallowing me any movement, but it doesn't cut off my air supply.

His mouth hovers inches from mine as he threatens in a deep tone. "For the last fucking time, it's Asher."

I'm about to speak when movement on my right catches my eye. A few students pass us by, openly gawking at the scene.

From their perspective, I'm standing on one leg, the other slightly bent. Asher's front is almost covering mine, and his hand is around my throat. No idea if it looks flirtatious or threatening.

But then again, Asher only appears threatening to me.

I place both hands on his T-shirt. The hard muscles ripple under my touch as I attempt to push him away.

He doesn't move. Not even an inch.

"People are staring," I hiss.

"Since when do you care?"

"Of course I care."

"No, you don't. Stop fucking around, Reina."

"I'm not fucking around." I lower my voice so no one hears. "I don't want to be seen being manhandled by you in public."

The corner of his lips tugs in a smirk. "Oh, but you have no say in that, remember? You're my property and I touch you whenever and however I damn fucking please."

The arrogance of this damn man. I'm tempted to punch him in the throat, but with his screwed up personality, he'll just hurt me tenfold worse.

So I choose a different approach. Swallowing all the profanities, I soften my tone. "You know, those who claim their *property* in public usually suffer from trust issues. Now, I'm sure that's not the case for you."

His expression remains neutral, but I know I got him. Considering the level of Asher's arrogance, I figured he wouldn't like to be accused of anything, let alone trust issues. Besides, he's the type who'd do everything to appear perfectly normal in the eyes of others. His perfect public image is everything he has and he'll protect it with all his might.

I wait for him to let me go, but his grip tightens.

No, no, no.

What…?

Hot breaths tickle my ear as his lips graze the sensitive shell. "That's where you're wrong. Do you know what I'm doing right now? I'm staking my claim in public so no one dares to trample with what's mine."

I suck in a breath, digging my fingers into his T-shirt. "People are watching."

"That's the point, my ugly monster."

"Ash—"

My words die at the back of my throat as his lips find the sensitive spot beneath my ear.

His lips latch onto the skin and he sucks it into his mouth. For someone as cold as Asher, his lips are burning hot. It's like I'm being set on fire and he won't stop until I turn to ashes.

Something unrestrained and wild grips me by the chest. The bottom of my stomach twists into itself, clawing and contracting as if it's about to fall.

My senses kick up in intensity and everything becomes heightened tenfold. The rustling of the nearby leaves. The stone of the wall digging into my back. The scent of the earth surrounding us. I can even hear the chirping of a bird in the distance.

My fingers curl into the cloth of his T-shirt. I meant to push him, but my hands remain there, colliding with his heartbeat.

The risk someone might be watching doesn't even sway me; if anything, it heightens my senses even more, as if that were possible.

Since the moment I woke up in the hospital, I've been a member of the walking dead, going through the motions like a robot. That's why depressive thoughts have been kicking in and dragging me into their merciless clutches.

Right now, as Asher ravishes my neck, it's the first time I've felt a burst of life running through me.

It hurts, you know.

Being dead for so long only to wake up all of a sudden hurts like a son of a bitch.

It's like a baby taking his first breath. The moment his lungs kick into gear, he bursts out crying.

That's what I feel like doing right now.

The rush of life is so strong I want to cry.

Asher's mouth trails from underneath my ear to the lobe. He bites it into his mouth, sucking and nibbling so hard I expect him to break the skin and feast on my veins like some vampire.

My head turns hazy and disoriented. It's like he's put me on a staircase and the more I climb, the higher I get.

For the first time since I woke up in the hospital, something feels right and yet so utterly wrong.

Whatever black magic he's performing on my skin is working. It's loosening my muscles and turning me into a liberated soul. I would've given anything to feel alive after waking up like the dead.

A moan rips from my throat, uncaring if anyone hears.

I feel his growl against my skin before I hear it.

Asher pulls back, chest rising and falling with his short breaths. His jaw ticks before he tucks his reaction away. "Why did you do that?"

"D-do what?" I'm genuinely confused.

"Moan." He says the word with distaste. "You don't moan."

What in the actual…?

"Am I not supposed to moan? Did I miss the memo somewhere?" I sound as perplexed as I feel.

"Who the fuck are you?" he asks with a semi-astonished tone as if seeing me for the first time.

"I'm…" I trail off. How the hell am I supposed to answer that question?

"You're nothing, Reina. You're only something

when I decide you are." He lowers his hand to my collarbone in a threatening caress. "Stop playing these fucking games with me."

"What games?" I'm panting. The skin where his mouth was feels like wild flames. "You're the one who trailed my ass and cornered me. Stop being so hot and cold, damn you."

"Hot and cold, huh?"

"Yes. You're giving me freaking whiplash, dude."

"*Dude*?" He tightens his hand around my neck as if he's pining for patience. "Oh, you're good. You've become so good at this. What will it be next? Spreading your legs for me?"

"You're the last person on this planet I would ever fuck." There isn't much conviction behind my words, but I stand my ground anyway.

"As if I would be interested in a monster like you."

I try to pretend it doesn't hurt. I try to ignore the pang creeping under my skin after how good he made me feel seconds ago.

The place he sucked on is turning ice cold all of a sudden. The fire has been extinguished and there are only ashes now.

I'm not the unfeeling monster he paints me as. It hurts, you know. Being this strongly hated and not knowing the reason pains me as much as my injuries.

Tears well in my eyes, but I blink them away. No one will see me weak and vulnerable.

No. One.

Instead, I puff up my chest. "Then why do you keep touching me?"

"I touch what's mine whenever I fucking please."

Anger bubbles under the surface, but I strike back in a cool tone. "Well, newsflash, Asher: I've decided I'm no longer yours. I'm calling off the engagement."

I'm surprised I lasted this long. I should've ended the whole thing when he called me a monster in the hospital.

This is another one of Old Reina's wrong decisions that I'm fixing for her.

You'll thank me later, girl.

True, she was the one who got engaged to him and she has the right to end it on her own. However, I can't possibly stay with this asshole when all he ever wants to do is hurt me.

I'm not that desperate.

Or fucking stupid.

He laughs, and the sound is as hollow as his soul. "That's not how it works."

"This is a free country. I won't stay engaged to a freak like you."

He watches me for long seconds as if my words fell

on deaf ears. "We've been engaged since we were fifteen. It's a family thing. Shut your mouth and go with it."

"Or what?"

"Or you lose the glamorous life you love so much." He tilts his head to the side. "The condition to receive your inheritance is to marry me." He leans in and brushes his tongue along the sensitive skin he sucked on earlier. "Till death do us part, my ugly monster."

Oh, no.

No, no, no.

Why the hell would my father do that?

My head becomes a jumbled mess. "But you obviously hate me. Why would you want to do this?"

Goosebumps cover my skin as he says, "You owe me a life, and I'll ruin yours as payback."

ASHER LEFT ME STANDING THERE.

Just like that. No *Do you need help getting inside?* Or anything remotely human.

Motherfucker.

I have to hobble for fifteen minutes to reach the entrance. Since I don't remember this place, it takes me even longer. I don't ask the others for help since that's the same as admitting weakness.

As soon as I walk through the huge doors, an onslaught of students greets me.

"You're okay, Reina?"

"How is the leg, Reina?"

"Is it true you were in a fire, Reina?"

"Are you cheering for the Devils this Friday?"

I try to smile, but it's like my reaction is frozen

beyond reach. I don't know these people, and while I'm glad no one seems to recognize I don't remember them, I don't want to sound or appear rude.

After all, this is my college.

The attention in the halls is like having a vicious tongue lap my skin. I can see hatred behind some smiles, envy behind others. There are also eager faces, both male and female, who wave awkwardly as if they're sure I won't return them.

I figured I'd be popular considering the stupid-ass cheerleading position, but I never thought it would be this...fake.

So far, I haven't met anyone who actually sees *me*, the person inside, not the face or the cheerleading uniform—though even I don't know who the hell the person inside is.

I focus on my steps instead of the horde of people surrounding me. The halls are large, but I can't breathe well with the crowd.

It's worse that I don't know where to go.

You should've planned this better.

Shut up, brain. I know that.

"Out of the way, fuckers," howls a familiar voice from the other side of the hall.

Students trip over each other to make way for none other than Owen.

He grins from ear to ear, winking at a girl here and smacking another's ass there. It's like he thinks he's a sex god blessing the peasants with his presence.

"Rei-Rei." His grin turns into a wicked one as he drapes an arm around my shoulder. "I thought you were going to be a zombie for a bit more."

"And I thought you'd stop being a pig by now."

"Define pig." He waggles an eyebrow. "Because if it means a lot of meat, then I do have that, babe."

"Eww. Gross."

His brows furrow and he pauses for a second. "You realize you just said that out loud, right?"

"Was I not supposed to?"

"Usually, I know you think it, but you never voice it."

"New person, new rules." I jab his hard, muscled side. "*Pig.*"

He laughs. "Well, shit. Looks like we got a new Rei-Rei in da house. You going to talk back to everything?"

"If you're being a little shit, why shouldn't I speak my mind?"

"Because you don't?" He waves two fingers in front of my face. "You usually have a blank robotic thing going on here."

"Why?"

"Don't know. Don't fucking care." He lifts a shoulder. "Now, about that BJ you promised me..."

"In your dreams, dude."

"Dude?" He stops, watching me closely.

Asher had a similar reaction when I called him that earlier.

"What's wrong with that?" I ask, unsure what the hell their problem is.

"You don't call me dude, Rei-Rei. Were you hit badly in the head?" He lifts a hand before I can form a response. "Don't answer. I don't care. I'm more interested in the BJ."

"I told you it's not happening, *dude*."

"Fine." He feigns a breath of resignation. "I'll settle for a lap dance."

"Hard pass."

His shoulders shake with laughter that somehow seems genuine compared to all the fakery I've seen since this morning.

"What was my reply when you asked me for blowjobs before?" I ask.

"You agreed, of course."

I narrow my eyes. For some reason, that doesn't ring true. "Don't lie to me."

"You really agreed." He squeezes my shoulder. "Didn't mean you did, though."

"Why the hell would I do that?"

He lifts a shoulder. "Beats me."

"What does…" I clear my throat. "How does Asher react to that? You're supposed to be his friend."

"Come on, of course he knows they don't happen. Otherwise, he would've been after my ass."

"And he's okay with the joking?"

"Meh. I thought so until he threatened me not to joke with you about BJs the other day." Owen shakes his head. "Weird son of a bitch."

Hmm. That's interesting.

We continue walking for a while. Deep down, I'm thankful for his presence. I would've felt utterly out of my element if Owen weren't by my side.

"What position do you play on the Devils?" I ask.

He raises an eyebrow as if he didn't expect me to ask that question. "Wide receiver."

"What about Sebastian?"

"Quarterback."

"Are you hoping to get drafted into the NFL?"

"What's with all these depressing questions first thing in the morning? You never gave two shits about us before."

"Oh."

I'm the head cheerleader so I figured both our teams

were one. After all, the cheerleading squad exists for the sake of the football team, no?

"I'm sorry." I meet Owen's brown gaze.

He stops in his tracks, and I'm forced to stop, too. "What did you just say?"

"I'm sorry I didn't care before."

He points a finger at me. "Who are you and what have you done with my bitchy Rei-Rei?"

Before I can answer that, a group of beautiful girls in cheerleading uniforms storm in our direction with Bree at the front. They pluck me away from Owen and surround me in one shallow hug after another.

They say things like they missed me and the team isn't the same without me. However, just like when the other students greeted me, I can sense a wicked undertone. If I'm being honest, some of the girls even appear sad I've returned.

Ouch. That stings.

At this rate, I'll end up with figurative needles all over my heart.

"Oh my Gosh, Reina"—Bree points at my shoes —"where did you get those vintage flats? Aren't they like five years out of fashion?"

I stare down at them, frowning. They're kind of cute. I mean, even the resident asshole, Asher, looked at them with amusement.

"They're back in style. Keep up, Bee," a girl on my right says in a bored tone.

She's wearing the cheerleading uniform and black-framed glasses that hide her Asian eyes. Black strands fall on either side of her face in slick lines like some anime character or a cosplay.

Now that I think about it, she's the only one who didn't hug me just now.

"It's *Bree*, not Bee," my supposed best friend bites out. "As if you'd ever know anything about fashion, Naomi."

The girl, Naomi, glares back. "I kind of do since my mom owns a fashion house and all that."

"Whatever." Bree brings out her phone and spends several minutes trying to fit everyone in a selfie frame.

I lean closer to Naomi and murmur, "Thanks."

"I didn't do it for you." She retrieves a tablet from her bag. "Bree is a bitch, but so are you."

She walks in the opposite direction before I can respond while Bree continues fussing with her phone.

"Never mind Naomi." A girl with a cute, goofy smile inches toward me. "She shouldn't even be with us. Dean George shoved her down our throats because her mom wouldn't give a generous donation to Blackwood College if her daughter isn't part of the cheerleading squad."

"Stop smiling like an idiot, Lucy," Bree snaps without looking back.

Lucy, the girl who was speaking to me, clamps her lips shut and slowly retreats.

Bree swings me to her side and orders several other girls, the prettiest ones, to stay back. She snaps several shots of the entire team. I try to smile for the picture, but the gutting fakery all around me is like tasting bitter acid.

She posts it on the cheerleading squad's Instagram account with the caption 'Captain is back!' then shows it to all of us. The girls *ooh* and *aah* for a while before their attention drifts to the latest gossip going around the college.

We walk down the hall. Bree and I are at the front, and the others follow like they're our ducklings or something.

This was my life? *Come on, Old Reina, you could've done better.*

Not that I'm judging or anything.

"Someone saw Jason Brighton outside this morning," one of the girls says over her gum.

Her friend gasps. "No way."

"Yes way." She pulls out her phone and opens an Instagram account with the handle devils-for-the-win. Sure enough, there's a picture of Jason's pickup truck pulling out from behind the college's student parking lot. Jeez. I can't believe someone managed to spot him even though he parked that far away.

"What's that loser doing here?" Bree snaps.

She has a squeaky kind of voice that really gets on my nerves. I'm tempted to hit her upside the head every time she talks that way. It's like she has zero respect for anyone.

Old Reina, why the hell were you even friends with her, let alone best friends?

Before I can come to Jason's defense, Lucy whispers, "Maybe he came to spy for the Knights."

"I'm sure that's not it—"

I'm cut off by a fuming Bree. "I'm going to tell the dean about this."

"There's no need," I tell her.

"What do you mean there's no need, Rei?" she scoffs. "They're our rivals and the game isn't far away. Do you want them to beat our asses?"

Okay, I definitely underestimated the whole rivalry thing between the Knights and the Devils. If the cheerleaders are so worked up about this, it must be huge.

In that case, it's better they don't know I asked Jason to drop me off. Obviously, the Knights aren't welcome around here.

Maybe that's why I kept my friendship with him secret?

I really *hope* that's the case and not some other snobbish reason.

"This is me." Bree leans in as if to kiss me, but she doesn't. She only says, "Muah, muah," on each side of my face and stalks off to class.

Things continue being awkward as the rest of the girls follow behind me. I test it and try to hobble faster, and they also quicken their pace. I walk slower, and they slow down, too.

Okay, this is ridiculous.

I stop and face them. "Walk beside me."

"Uh…we don't do that." Lucy bites her cheek.

"You and Bree are always in front," another says.

"Well, that changes now. I'm not your mama duck." My attempt at humor falls on deaf ears. They watch me with quizzical expressions, and none of them laugh.

I shake my head. "Just come over here."

One by one, the girls abandon their backup-dancer positions and trickle to my sides.

Lucy takes my right, grinning until her nose scrunches. We round the corner in silence. Students keep staring at us—or maybe they're staring at me.

"Rei…" Lucy starts. "I mean, I know you probably

don't want to talk about it, but the girls are so curious about what happened."

"I don't remember."

"Oh, right." Lucy exchanges a look with the others, as if they expected me to say that.

"I *really* don't remember."

"Yeah, sure, Reina." Lucy's grin falls a little. "It's just that we were so worried when we heard the police found human remains close to where you were attacked."

I come to a screeching halt, forcing the entire squad to stop, too. "How do you know about that?"

"D-Dad is the deputy commissioner. I'm sorry."

"Don't be." I frown. This is my chance to know what happened back there. "Do you remember the night I disappeared?"

"Of course I do." She grins. "We played against the Vikings."

"And beat their asses," a girl adds. "Do you remember Seb's last-minute play?"

"Totally cool," Lucy says before facing me. "You disappeared before the end of our routine."

"I did?"

"Yeah. I remember it so well because you never do that. You're usually the last one to leave."

That means I broke a pattern. There's definitely

something fishy about that night. "Do you know where I went?"

They all shake their heads, and Lucy says, "We thought you snuck out with Asher since he came back from England that weekend."

He's obviously mad I disappeared on him that night. There's no way I went to see him, which leaves one option.

Did you think you could escape?

I'm beginning to believe maybe Asher's assumptions are true. Maybe, just maybe, I planned to disappear from Blackwood for good.

Now, I have to figure out why.

CHAPTER 11 - REINA

DEAN GEORGE personally welcomes me back to the college. I don't know if I should feel honored or awkward, so I settle on something in the middle.

Awkward smile.

He only leaves after he makes sure I'm settled in the cafeteria and have my plate of food in front of me.

We have an entire long table for the cheerleading and football teams, but the football team has a meeting with their coach so it's only us for now.

Some male cheerleaders join us, but just like the girls, they seem more wary than happy to see me.

"Does the dean welcome all his students back? I thought he would be a busy man considering the size of this college." I grab a bottle of water as I watch him disappear down the hall. His assistant nearly falls on her face trying to keep up with him.

Naomi, the Asian girl from earlier, bursts out laughing as she stabs her fork into her pizza.

I pause in opening the bottle. "Why are you laughing?"

"Ignore her," Bree says in a dramatic voice while picking at her salad.

My meal is also a salad. Apparently, we only eat salad on this squad—except for Naomi. I eye the pizza on all the other students' plates and my mouth waters. I'd kill to have a slice.

I meet Naomi's icy stare with my own. "Tell me why you're laughing."

"You must've really hit your head so hard, *queen*." She says the last bit with pure mockery.

"Shut it, Naomi," Bree scolds.

"No, let her speak." I smile, crossing my arms over the table. "We're a team, right? You can tell me anything."

"God, I can't believe this," Naomi huffs. "Well, Queen Bitch—that's your name around here, by the way—your daddy and your sugar daddy pay a shitload of money to this college. If you asked the dean to crawl on all fours like a dog, he'd be woofing."

"That's enough! You're out, Naomi." Bree hisses as all the girls—and even the boys—grow silent.

All clinks of utensils come to a halt, and everyone holds their breath.

Their wild eyes swing back to mine, as if expecting me to transform into a raging bull and squash Naomi under my boot –or in my case, flats.

I do no such thing and just watch the scene like an outsider looking in.

This was my life.

I'm a queen bitch and my teammates are scared of me.

Old Reina, just what the hell were you?

"Whatever." Naomi jerks up, swinging her messenger bag over her shoulder. She yanks her plate off the table and stomps out of the cafeteria.

"I'm so going to teach that bitch a lesson," Bree mutters under her breath.

"Calm down, Bree." Prescott, one of the male cheerleaders, pats her arm, and she shoves him away.

"What's Naomi's problem with me?" I ask no one in particular.

"Uh…nothing." Lucy slides to my side, grinning. "She's just still bitter about the prank we pulled on her last year."

"What prank?"

Lucy's plump cheeks turn crimson, but she says nothing.

"Lucy." I level her with a determined glare. "Tell me."

"Uh…you dared Sebastian Weaver to fuck her."

"She's been mad at all of us ever since," Prescott adds.

"As in more bitchy and grumpier than usual," another girl, Morgan, says.

"She doesn't even eat low carb like the rest of us."

"And she doesn't run in the mornings either."

"Have you seen her thighs? Or those saggy arms?"

"Someone saw her sleeping in a cemetery. How creepy is that?"

God. These girls are like vapid animals tearing their prey's flesh apart while laughing and joking.

The boys continue eating in silence, but it's the same as participating.

I ignore them, focusing on Naomi holding her plate and storming out of the cafeteria. Her steps are tense and her shoulders hunch with tension.

Did I do that to her? Did I turn her into someone hated by her own team?

In my understanding, being the captain means taking care of the entire squad. Why do I feel like it's been the other way around?

How could I dare someone to fuck with such a cute girl like Naomi?

I stand up, wiping my mouth with a napkin. My appetite for this salad is non-existent anyway.

"Where are you going, Rei?" Bree places a hand on my arm as if demanding I sit back down. "We have to go through our routine, remember?"

No, I don't remember. That's the entire fucking problem.

Still, I offer them the slight smile I'm starting to think they expect of me. "I'll be back."

Not putting too much pressure on my hurt leg, I make a beeline out of the cafeteria, nodding and smiling at anyone who calls my name. A redheaded boy who can't be any older than a sophomore freezes when I wave back at him.

Goddammit. Please tell me I wasn't the type who belittled everyone around her.

Old Reina, I'm seriously starting to hate you.

Outside, I spot Naomi retreating to the back entrance of the college. I hobble my way after her and stop near a fountain that has a Greek-like statue on top.

Naomi sits at the edge and slams the plate on her lap. A few football players wearing the Devils' black and white jackets head in the direction of the cafeteria. They must've finished their meeting.

Owen and Sebastian are there, too, deep in conversation with their teammates.

The moment Sebastian notices Naomi, he abandons his friends and joins her on the edge of the fountain.

The jerk does it with ease, too, as if he's entitled to invade her space. True, he's good-looking with golden hair and sun-kissed skin, and from what I've heard, he's the star quarterback, but so what?

I stand on one leg but lean over to hear what they're talking about.

"Hey, tsundere." He grins. "What type of trouble are you up to today?"

She doesn't raise her head from her plate, as if she's still all alone. "Beating your ass into the fountain or shoving your face up your ass. Take your pick."

Sebastian laughs and bumps her shoulder with his. "I knew you were kinky. Tell me more."

"Fuck off."

"I would rather fuck on." He winks.

"What part of leave me alone do you not understand? I hate you, asshole."

"But I don't."

She grabs her plate and attempts to leave.

"You don't have to play so hard to get, tsundere." He taps her nose. "You're just a fuck, remember?"

Naomi turns as red as a tomato as he stands up and stalks back toward his friends.

Jerk.

No wonder he's Asher's friend. The asshole surrounds himself with dipshits who resemble him.

But then again, I'm the one who dared Sebastian. That part is all on me.

I limp to Naomi's side, my head lowered and my skin prickling with shame.

"For the last time, I won't suck you off. I'd rather eat vomit off the walls," she snaps.

"Wow. That's quite the visual." I smile.

Her head jerks up and her gaze immediately hardens. "You."

"Yeah, me." I sit down beside her, keeping some distance between us. "Do you mind?"

"I do, actually. I escaped your band of mean girls to eat in peace."

"But Sebastian ruined it."

Her upper lip lifts in disgust. "Screw that asshole."

"Yeah, screw him with a backward stick so he feels pain every time he thinks about screwing someone." I smile tentatively. "I'm sure this is too late, but I wanted to say I'm so sorry for that dare."

She raises an eyebrow as if not believing what I just said. "Is this some sort of reverse psychology where you'll get me to admit my deepest darkest secrets and wishes? You don't have to, because my wish already didn't come true."

"How so?"

"I wished you'd die, but you're still alive."

"Oh."

My heart sinks as I stare at my flats with my hands in my lap. I didn't think she hated me to the point of wishing me dead.

Old Reina, what have you done?

"Shit. You're really upset?" Naomi watches me closely. "I never thought I'd live to see Reina Ellis upset."

"Of course I get upset, I'm a human."

"More like a monster who survives on being cunning, manipulating others, and screwing people's lives over." Her rapid-fire words stab me right in the chest.

Asher isn't the only one who thinks I'm a monster. Is that my nickname in everyone's subconscious?

"I told you I'm sorry, didn't I?" I say hopefully.

"Sorry? Do you think sorry fixes *anything*?" She laughs with a bitter edge as she stands up. "You can take your sorry and shove it up your skinny ass."

And then she's storming out of view.

My shoulders droop as I angle sideways and stare at my reflection in the water.

Who knew behind such a beautiful face lurked a nightmare?

I should've had a purpose, right? But no matter how much I think about it, there can't possibly be an excuse to hurt people.

It's just wrong. Everything is so wrong.

Another beautifully cruel face greets me in the reflection before he throws a rock in the water, disturbing both our images.

I turn around and scowl at Asher's face, which is still covered by aviators.

Does he ever remove them?

His broad shoulders block the sun and his shadow falls over me like damnation.

Izzy said Asher played football in high school, but unlike his friends, he chose to study international law.

Why would he abandon that now? We spent three years apart; why would he come back now of all times?

He makes less sense than my missing memories.

"Do you believe how much of a monster you are now?" he asks with a cool edge.

I fold my arms. "I know why Naomi hates me. Why don't you tell me why you hate me?"

"Why?" He leans forward, filling the air with his sheer presence. "So you can kiss it better?"

"Sure, why not?" I taunt.

"Reina," he growls.

I have learned a trick when it comes to dealing with Asher: if I cower, he'll push until I fall, but if I push back, he's taken by surprise.

People like Asher are easier to handle when they're caught off guard. It's impossible to clash with him when he has all his walls up. It'll just destroy my armor.

"Did I make you do a dare, too?" I place a hand on his T-shirt, my voice dramatic. "You didn't like the girl?"

He snatches my wrist and holds it in a deadly grip. "Stop fucking around, or you'll regret it."

What's there to regret when I already hate my life?

I lean closer and whisper in his ear, "Show me your worst, Ash."

ON MY SECOND day back at college, Bree invites me to join them for practice, but I pass.

She glances at me with a frown, the kind everyone seems to be giving me since I woke up in the hospital.

"Whatever, Rei," she scoffs on her way out of a psychology lecture. "It's not like we're competing for state or anything."

I pause gathering my books as everyone throws curious glances our way. I swear a phone flashed as if taking a picture of me.

"I just don't see what I could add when I can barely walk," I say slowly.

Truth is, I'm scared about facing the whole cheer-leading thing. What if all that was wiped clean with my memories? If I can't remember who I am or why I did all those awful things, how can I remember flipping in the air? I've seen videos of myself on the squad's YouTube channel. I'm one of those who gets thrown and flips in the air before landing at the top. That shit is scary.

Bree closes in on me. The other cheerleaders who are in the same class stand behind her as if they're scared of what's about to go down.

"Team spirit, Reina." She grips the edge of the table hard until her knuckles turn white.

One of the students elbows his friend on their way out.

Bree clears her throat and lowers her voice. "You have to get your shit together or I swear to God…"

"What?" I insist when she trails off. "If you start a threat, finish it."

"Karma, Reina." She straightens. "That always comes around to bite you in the ass."

She flips her hair and storms out of the classroom.

I stand there, clutching my bag and feeling completely out of my element.

My head nearly explodes from the number of scenarios running rampant in it. Could I have wronged Bree, too?

Honestly, with my track record, I wouldn't be surprised.

Naomi breezes past me with a vindictive smirk on her face.

"Hashtag bitch fight." She blows her gum into a bubble and pops it in my face. I close my eyes, pining for patience. The only reason I'm not attacking her is because I've done something unforgivable.

"Leave Captain alone." Lucy stands in front of me protectively.

Naomi flips her off. "Gladly, follower." She starts to leave then stops and throws another comment over her shoulder. "Oh, and Luce, you might want to pick that up."

Lucy looks around, confused. "What?"

"Your dignity." And then Naomi is out the door.

Lucy sniffles. I stand up on a wobbly leg and awkwardly pat her shoulder. I'm totally unsure when it comes to comforting others, but I hate seeing Lucy in pain.

I've only known her for two days, but she and Naomi are easily the most non-fake people in the squad. She makes sure to fill me in whenever I'm lost. She's not a follower like Naomi called her; she's just doing her best to have everyone get along.

She's a pacifier. Mom used to tell me those types usually have a soft, breakable core.

Wait…

Mom?

How can I remember what Mom told me? I thought I didn't have a mom.

I mean, of course I was birthed by one, but she died during childbirth. From what I've gathered about my life—through Google—my dad has been a single parent all his life, so there isn't a possibility of a stepmom either.

"Oh, I'm sorry, Captain." Lucy wipes the moisture underneath her eyes. "I won't do it again."

"Do what?" I sound as confused as I feel.

"You told us not to cry in public or you'd have us clean the toilet."

Holy shit. I was a dictator.

"Forget about that." I offer her my handkerchief, and she takes it like it's the Holy Grail. "You don't have to defend me, Lucy. I can stand up for myself just fine."

"I just didn't want it to get out of hand between you two. Nao can be really vindictive."

"Nao?" I raise a brow. "She lets you call her that?"

"Ugh. Old habits. We used to be friends. Best friends, actually."

"What happened?"

"She hates me since the whole Seb thing. She thinks I knew and didn't tell her and that I betrayed her." She lifts a shoulder. "Doesn't matter."

God, I feel as evil as Hitler. Wait, maybe I *was* Hitler in a previous life. After all, we're both dictators with a tendency for craziness.

"I'm so sorry, Luce." I squeeze her arm lightly.

She stares with wide eyes, her jaw nearly hitting the floor.

"Lucy?" I wave a hand in front of her face. Shit, I think I broke the poor girl.

"Uh…yeah…sorry. It's just…we studied together since high school and that's the first time I've heard you apologize."

"Don't be silly. Everyone apologizes."

"Not you, Reina. You don't do apologies, you don't offer me your handkerchief, and you sure don't stay back to make sure any of us are fine."

Bile rises to my throat as her words strike me like a whip. I was fake. Vain. Selfish.

A shell.

The worst type of person to ever exist.

The thought hurts more than I'd like to admit. It's like perching over a snow globe and watching myself. From the outside looking in, I had the perfect face and body. I had the grades and the cheerleading squad. I had Dad's fortune and Alex's endless support.

But if I look closer, I see a trapped girl. A hollow life.

A nothingness.

Maybe Asher was right to call me a monster.

That gloomy cloud creeps over me and crawls over my skin.

Disgusting.

You're disgusting.

You should die.

"Are you okay?" Lucy asks.

I force myself out of my head and fake a smile. "I'm fine."

"Don't let what Bree said get to you. She's thinking about the team. Without you, our spirits were pretty low, you know."

No, I don't know. Why the hell is someone like me popular amongst these girls? I'm not an example they should look up to.

I'm everything they need to avoid.

"I'll go with you," I tell Lucy.

Her eyes light up like a Christmas tree. "You will?"

I interlink my arm with hers and she freezes, her body going tense. I pull back just as fast. Apparently, I didn't use to do that, and if I keep giving her too many surprises, she might break for real this time.

On our way to the gym, my skin prickles with unwanted attention. At first I think it's the usual students gawking at me.

It never stops—the attention, the waves, the fake greetings. Today, I contemplated covering my head and remaining in bed.

The only reason I didn't is because my head scares me. If I stay alone with it, I'll be doomed. I'll take the fake flattery over that gloomy cloud any day.

Lucy nudges me, giggling under her breath. When I follow her field of vision, my ears heat.

Asher.

My eyes find him of their own volition. I don't even need to search for him anymore. It's crazy how much his presence draws me in.

Sometimes, I think I'm still that lifeless form in the hospital and he's the one who breathed life into me.

Sure, it's a toxic life, sinister and dark, but it's life all the same.

The weird awareness of his presence must be because he's the reason behind my return to life.

Delusional much, Reina?

He seems to be out on a run since he's wearing a sleeveless T-shirt and shorts. Lucy tells me he's been practicing with the track team since he returned, but it's not official.

I'm not listening to her.

My focus is on the tattoo lines snaking over the top of his bicep, rippling with every step he takes.

The T-shirt is glued to his six-pack like a second skin. His damp hair sticks to his forehead. The dark strands are begging to be pushed back, gripped, combed.

A few guys walk on either side of him, but he doesn't seem focused on them. Since his aviators are gone, I can finally see his expression.

His eyes are lost in an indifferent zone, like nothing really matters to him. It's so similar to my gloomy cloud, which tells me to just let go.

It says there's no use in being here.

Maybe Asher doesn't like people to see that expression. Is that why he wears sunglasses all the time?

Except, well, he's usually friendly with everyone around him—except with me.

It could be he's putting up a façade, too. I always catch myself faking smiles in front of the squad and everyone at school.

Asher's dark eyes meet mine, and my world shifts for a second.

How can a look hold so many promises and threats and…something else I can't identify?

A slow humming starts at my spine and twists the bottom of my stomach. This is what it feels like to be caught in someone's orbit.

It's dangerous. It's wrong. It's…thrilling.

My gaze finds his mouth, that warm mouth that isn't as cold as the rest of him. I'm taken back to that time when those lips and teeth and tongue were all over my neck, my ears.

Me.

I cut off eye contact and quicken my pace to the gym.

Still, my body temperature won't go down, and my heart beats as if I were the one running.

In the gym, Prescott and the other guys are practicing some throws with the girls. Bree stands at the head, huffing and screaming at them to do better.

Everyone pauses upon my entrance, and Bree stares back with an impatient look. When she sees me, her brows scrunch together. "You're here."

"I am."

"You should've seen her with Asher just now," Lucy says in a dreamy voice. "You guys are the best couple ever. You can feel the chemistry in the air."

"That's not true!" I shout as if she spoke blasphemy.

"Shut it, Luce." Bree snaps her fingers. "Go warm up."

The latter ducks her head and heads to the locker room.

"Stop being so mean to her," I tell Bree, crossing my arms.

"Mean? What are you talking about?"

It's like this is a normal occurrence. Hell, I could've been exactly like her in the past.

Bree inches toward me but keeps her hawk-like gaze on the team. "So, who's the target of our next dare?"

"No one," I say loud enough for everyone to hear. "That nonsense will end now."

She laughs but leans in to hiss, "Even you can't change the rules, Reina."

A flash stabs my head as a memory invades my senses.

We shouldn't have broken the rules, Reina.

I SIT CROSS-LEGGED on the rooftop of the college and cradle a plate on my lap.

My gaze gets lost in the buildings that extend all over the city. It's not exactly beautiful, but it's ancient.

Like the entire college.

Blackwood is a few centuries old, and this has always been one of the top towns for business and for rich people like Alex—and my dad.

Oh, and the mafia people who worked with my dad.

Since that van incident, I haven't noticed anyone trailing after me. After I told Alex about it, he told me to always stay in crowds.

Just because they're gone doesn't mean they won't come back, Reina.

His last words shoot terror down my spine. Still, I need a breather from the fakery sometimes.

A week has come and gone. Every day I go to college and pretend today will be better.

Today, I won't hate Old Reina.

It's proving to be an epic failure. The more I get to know the girl from before, the more intense my existential crisis becomes.

That's probably why I snuck up here all alone. It's hard since the squad won't stop following me all over campus.

Sitting here on my own feels a tad liberating. I can breathe without feeling a constant weight on my chest.

I stab my fork at my plate. It's chicken today. Not great, but still way better than salad.

Another reason for my mood is last night's dream— or was it a nightmare?

I held someone's arm and kept running like we were escaping death. It was so dark, I couldn't see whose hand I was holding, but I could feel our connection. I felt safe with that person, like we could fly to the moon and swim amongst the stars.

Then suddenly, they let go of my hand. I screamed, but no sound came out. Then something hit the back of my neck and I woke up with a start.

I can't stop thinking about that dream. No idea if it's a figment of my imagination or a memory.

Let's hope it's the first, because I don't want that person hurt.

I might not have seen them, but my heart remembers them. It's been aching non-stop since I woke up.

Losing my appetite, I push the plate away and lie on my back. I couldn't care less if my skirt and shirt get dirty.

Nothing really matters now.

The only bright spot this week was removing my leg brace. I can walk without it just fine now. The bruises have started to fade, too.

I stare at the afternoon sun in the middle of the sky and lift my hand as if I can reach it.

Maybe if I can, I'll box it up and use it whenever that gloomy cloud takes control of my head.

I have classes in the afternoon, but I just don't care about them, or about my fake friends.

So I just close my eyes and let the sun soak me.

"We're weaker when we're apart."
"So we just have to be together."
"We can't."
"No…"

"Promise me you'll protect yourself. Even if I'm not there, you'll be safe."

"No, Reina. No."

"I'll be safe, too. We'll meet again. Promise."

"I promise."

I'm thrown back to the present with a shove. I stand on the edge, nearly falling down. That's when I realize I'm *literally* on the edge.

My surroundings have turned pitch black, but I recognize the college's towers and the town's lights in the distance.

I remember coming up to the roof and closing my eyes, then...what?

Why the hell am I standing on the ledge?

My arms are bound behind my back and duct tape covers my mouth. The rope is tied to a pole behind me and my whole body is angled forward as if I'm about to free-fall from the roof.

The reality of my situation hits me like a violent storm.

I shriek, but the sound is muted by the duct tape.

Closing my eyes, I breathe deeply. This must be a nightmare. I'm trapped in a nightmare.

I slowly open my eyes, and the darkness grips me

by the throat again. Like a savage animal, it claws at my skin and crunches my bones.

The ground is so far away. If the ropes fail, my skull will be crushed to pieces. There are no people in sight.

I'm going to fall.

I'm going to die.

No.

Not now. I didn't survive this long to die now.

Panic won't help me. Not at all. I grip the rope with both hands and drag my unsteady leg on the solid edge.

The pole creaks behind me. The ropes loosen, moving me farther out.

I lose my footing and scream. My nails dig into the rope and I hold on to it with all my might.

My fingers scrape, and a hot liquid trickles from underneath my nails.

Air suffocates me and I can't breathe. For a moment, I let that gloomy cloud take over my mind.

Why don't you let the rope drop you?

Why don't you die?

I shake my head furiously, inhaling shaky breaths.

In my dream, I made a promise to that female voice not to die.

Slowly, I inch my leg to the edge, clenching the rope in a death grip. The material scratches against my bloody nails.

My senses heighten and every little sound registers in my ears: the squeaking of the shaky pole, the desperate drag of my leg to the solid edge, the roaring pulse of my heartbeat.

I attempt to sit down. My leg nearly slips, and the ropes tighten around my wrists. I stop, sucking in a shaky breath.

Carefully, I stand back up with one of my legs suspended in the air.

This is it. I have to rip it off like a Band-Aid.

Inhaling deeply, I claw at the rope with my nails and push myself back.

The loud squeak of the pole registers first.

Then the loosening of the rope.

Tears fill my eyes as my entire body leans downward, toward my imminent fall.

I'm so sorry I couldn't keep my promise.

I'm so sorry.

A brute force pulls me back by the rope. My body jerks to the edge and the bindings tighten around my wrists due to the power.

I topple over and fall into a solid embrace.

Cold, but also warm.

Hard, but also safe.

My heart, which was ready to die a second ago, resurrects back to life with a shocking force.

I gasp for air as if I haven't been breathing for days or months.

The need to cry hits me like a hurricane. I'm caught in the eye of the storm, begging for some sort of release.

Blinking away the tears, I stare up at my savior, the one whose arms surround me like a cage.

He has the most beautiful eyes, my savior. Green like a dark forest, but also like a tropical sea during a storm.

He's a dream and a nightmare, my savior, like darkness and light.

He's Asher.

CHAPTER 14 - G

SHE LOOKS her best when she's hanging by a rope.
Bound and exposed.

Stripped bare.

I admire my handiwork: the knot around her wrists,
the duct tape on her mouth.

My dick becomes hard thinking about fucking her
in that position.

Will she cry? Will she beg?

My dick has to wait, though.

Reina Ellis' nightmare is far from over.

THE FOLLOWING DAY, I don't go to class.

I don't know how I got back to the house last night. I vaguely remember Asher carrying me, and that's it.

He asked me who did it, but I found no words. If I'd said anything, I would've let the tears loose. I chose silence instead.

Silence is safe sometimes.

Silence is also when the gloomy cloud strikes. You can feel it, you know, those thoughts occupying your mind and refusing to come out.

Thoughts like last night's.

I felt that yearning to fall and end it all—but Asher stopped it. He…breathed life into me again—against my will.

I didn't know how much I needed life until my heart kicked into gear, its beat filling my whole being.

It was almost as if it screamed at me to stay alive.

To ignore the gloomy cloud.

So today, I decided to do just that. The pull to remain in bed all day grips me like a vengeful ghost, but I manage to push the covers off and stand, to shower and freshen up.

The only thing I can't do is look at myself in the mirror.

Baby steps.

I come down the stairs around ten. I stop in the vast living area with all its flawless marble and sweeping staircase. For some reason, it feels vacant and so...wrong.

Wrong place. Wrong life.

Those thoughts from when I first woke up at the hospital assault me again.

I flop down on a chesterfield sofa. The need to lie down and sleep surrounds me like a lullaby, but I don't surrender to it.

A disaster happened the last time I did that.

Who would do that to me and why?

If I want to find answers, I need to know more about myself.

I pull out my phone and google my name. Several

pictures come up, in cheerleading uniforms, at fundraisers alongside Alex, and at parties.

The smile on my face is so sickening and fake. I hate that smile. It's not me.

There are a few articles about my disappearance for a month when I was twelve, some speculate there was a kidnapping. Others say, it was a runaway case. The picture where I was shot as Dad held me showed me in dirty clothes, my hair in a disarray and my face blank – so blank it's frightening.

I run my fingers over the picture. "What happened to you back then?"

Dad's name appears as a related search: Gareth Ellis. I googled him before and spent hours looking at his pictures. They always brought me a sense of safety and calm.

Gareth Ellis was a tall, fit man like Alex. He has that all-American look with blond hair, bright blue eyes, and a squarish jawline. He always wore English-cut suits like he was born in one.

I run my fingers along his face, feeling the pressure building behind my eyes.

Miss you, Papa.

According to his Wikipedia page, Dad was a bachelor his entire life. There isn't a single picture of his wife—my mother—anywhere. No matter how much I dig, I only come up with gossip articles speculating that my mother could be a whore my dad impregnated.

My nose scrunches. From what I've gathered about Dad so far, he was never caught in a scandal about women. In an article, he told them, "I have the only girl I need by my side, my Rei."

I close the search results so I don't start bawling like an idiot. What right do I have to grieve my dad when I don't even remember him?

My finger hovers over Instagram before I open it. My profile is as plastic as my life.

It's all about rallies, cheerleading, and partying with the rest of the squad. My selfies are perfection incarnate with perfect makeup and perfect settings and perfect everything.

Sometimes, Owen and Sebastian take pictures with me, which should mean we've kept in touch over the past three years.

I scroll farther to my oldest pictures. Considering I'm an attention whore who posts often, it takes me several minutes to reach memories from high school.

My only picture with Asher stares back at me. It's three years old, which means we were seniors at the time.

He stands in the middle of the empty field wearing white and blue football gear. His jersey sticks to his abs with sweat, and black lines sit underneath his eyes accentuating their forest color.

He grins in a wide and slightly cocky way, appearing every bit the gorgeous bastard he is.

He carries me bridal style in his strong arms. I'm wearing a matching white and blue cheerleading uniform with 'Blue Tigers' written on top. One of my legs is tossed high in the air as both my arms form a V with blue pom-poms.

Friday night lights shine behind us, creating a picture-perfect couple. There's no caption, but there are hashtags.

#TigersForTheWin #We'reTheBest #StateHereWe-Come #MyHero

I gawk at the last hashtag as if I can get into my head at the time and figure out why the hell I called him that.

Then I watch my smile in the picture. Wide and goofy, almost…happy. It's not fake like all my smiles afterward. If anything, my picture with Asher is the last one where I had a resemblance of a genuine smile. Everything after that is plastic, dishonest…fake.

What happened three years ago?

I attempt to stalk Asher's social media and see if the change is mutual. Then I recall Lucy telling me he doesn't use social media. He never did, not even in high school.

I wonder why.

I check my DMs. They're all either from Bree or the rest of the squad. They're asking why I'm not answering my phone and haven't returned to school.

I only reply to Lucy, telling her I have a doctor's appointment.

Hopefully she believes it and asks the others to leave me alone.

I'm about to exit Instagram when a new message pops up on my screen. The username is Cloud003. I click on it out of curiosity then gasp.

Cloud003: Do you want to know who bound you like a slut?

My heartbeat picks up as I read and re-read the message. Is this the person who did it?

I scroll up and find other messages from the same user.

The first one he sent was two years ago.

Cloud003: I enjoyed your pussy tonight. Happy Halloween.

Cloud003: By the way, that mask you wore was such a lousy disguise. I obviously know who you are.

Reina-Ellis: What makes you think I don't know who you are too?

Cloud003: Doubtful. Otherwise, you wouldn't have opened your legs for me so readily. You wouldn't have come that hard on my cock. Admit it—you like the thrill of the unknown.

Reina-Ellis: So do you.

Cloud003: But I already know who you are, my slut. Are you my slut, Reina?

Reina-Ellis: I am.

Cloud003: Only my slut?

Reina-Ellis: Only yours.

I gawk at the messages. That can't be possible. I would never call myself a slut.

Besides, who the hell is this guy?

I click on his profile. It's set on private and there's no profile picture. He has zero followers and follows two accounts, but I can't see what they are.

Dammit.

I go back to the exchange between us.

After that exchange, there was a message from me.

Reina-Ellis: Can we meet?

Cloud003: That's not how it works, Reina. Repeat it and say it right this time.

Reina-Ellis: Can we meet, please?

Cloud003: I love it when you beg, but no, I'm not interested in you outside the unknown.

Reina-Ellis: But you already know who I am.

Cloud003: Exactly.

Reina-Ellis: You're a jerk.

Cloud003: One whose cock you rode all night.

Reina-Ellis: Screw you. I'm not talking to you anymore.

No more messages came from him until a year later, last fall, in October.

Cloud003: I knew you would change your mind, my slut.

Reina-Ellis: I didn't.

Cloud003: Then why did you come to the same Halloween party dressed in the same kitten mask?

Reina-Ellis: I didn't come to this party because of you.

Cloud003: Is that why you keep watching me from across the room when you think I'm not looking?

Reina-Ellis: Fuck you.

Cloud003: I would rather fuck you.

Cloud003: Get your ass to the same room in five

minutes. When I walk in there, I want you fully naked on your back, your legs spread wide apart. Don't turn on any lights or I'll go.

Cloud003: Leave the mask and the heels on.

Reina-Ellis: What makes you think I want to fuck you?

Cloud003: Four minutes, Reina.

Reina-Ellis: Jerk.

Cloud003: One who'll be fucking that tight pussy all night.

A day later, there's a message from me.

Reina-Ellis: You still don't want to meet?

Cloud003: No.

Reina-Ellis: Why not?

Cloud003: Don't you have a fiancé?

Reina-Ellis: He doesn't matter. I'm your slut, remember?

Cloud003: And that's all you'll ever be. Don't ask for more or you'll regret it. See you next year.

I stare at the words as if I'm learning to read. The evidence of my infidelity stares back at me with ugly, disgusting words.

What the hell have I done?

No more messages were exchanged between Cloud003 and me until a day before my accident.

Reina-Ellis: I won't meet you again.

Cloud003: Nice try, my slut.

Reina-Ellis: I mean it. I'm turning the page and you chose not to be part of it. I know you're blocking any feelings you have for me and I understand. I probably should've done the same. I'm sorry and goodbye.

He didn't reply. The only other message is the one I just received.

How does he know I was bound to the roof last night? My first knee-jerk reaction is to ask him if he's the one who did it.

I stop myself at the last second. He could be a psycho. Scratch that, he's most likely a psycho.

It's better not to engage with them. Besides, I clearly told him goodbye.

My heart somersaults in my chest as my screen lights up with another message.

Cloud003: Be careful, my slut. Someone is after your life. I'd hate to see those beautiful eyes vacant.

CHAPTER 16 - G

I LEAN BACK in my seat and watch her rosy cheeks through the camera.

The way she bites her lower lip as she stares at the phone.

The way her slender body straightens, her tits straining against her cotton T-shirt.

She's beautiful and she knows it.

Maybe that's why she chose to be a bitch queen.

I reach for my dick and readjust it.

Blackwood will soon have another tragedy.

Reina will play the main role.

FOR THE NEXT THREE DAYS, I go to college, but I barely concentrate on anything. I keep watching my phone, expecting Cloud003 to send me another text.

He doesn't.

I should be thankful, but the unknown is killing me. At night, I re-read our exchanges and contemplate reaching out to him. He probably doesn't know I lost my memories, and I could indulge him to get information.

But what if he knows and I put myself in danger?

My self-preservation instinct is better than that.

I push the door open and sigh heavily.

"Hey, Izzy." I greet her as she carries grocery bags into the kitchen.

"Oh, you're back," she says with a bit of surprise in her tone.

"Am I not supposed to be?"

"You usually spend as much time as possible out before coming home."

The squad did invite me to go out, but I wasn't feeling it. I went with them yesterday, and it ruined my mood instead of lifting it.

"What are you going to do?" I motion at the grocery bags.

"Bake."

My mood brightens. Finally something out of the ordinary. "Can I join?"

She completely freezes as if I just drove a knife into her heart. She blinks three times. "You...want to join me."

"That's what I said."

"To bake?"

I nod.

"In the kitchen?"

"Is that so weird to ask?"

"It's just you never step foot in the kitchen."

"Well, that's Old Reina. I'm a new person now." I say the words louder than needed, as if I need to convince myself.

Every day I spend at college, I discover the atrocities the old me did. Even if I want to change, I can't possibly undo what I did in the past.

Or can I?

Redemption is so hard when you don't know where or how to start.

With a deep breath, I follow Izzy to the kitchen. The vast area is filled with stainless steel appliances and white marble.

"Must be a bitch to clean all this white," I tell Izzy as she busies herself behind the counter.

"Tell me about it." She pauses. "I mean, I'm fine with it."

"You don't have to watch what you say, Izzy. I swear nothing will get back to Alex." I make a motion of zipping my mouth, locking it, and tossing the imaginary key out the window.

Her kind eyes crinkle on the sides with a smile. "It's like you're an entirely new person."

"A better one?" My tone holds so much hope, it's pathetic.

She nods. "Well, yes. You're more vocal, and less…"

"Snobby," I finish for her. "I know. I kind of figured that out."

She smiles awkwardly, and we silently agree to let the subject go.

We get to work. Izzy prepares the dough and speaks about Jason and the NFL draft. It's their dream coming true.

My heart warms at how proud she is of him, but also at the sacrifices she's made to get him here. When her husband died, leaving Izzy with a toddler, she moved from the south to escape her conservative family after they tried to force her into marrying a man 'to take care of her'. She worked several jobs until she got to Alex's house.

"Jason is lucky to have a mother like you," I tell her as I shape the cookie dough with her.

"I'm lucky to have him as my son." She grins.

"Izzy?" I don't meet her eyes as I ask. "Since you've been here for a long time, have you ever met my mom?"

She shakes her head in my peripheral vision. "When I came to work here, your dad was your only parent."

"Then have you ever heard anything about her?"

"I think she died during childbirth? That's what I heard from the servants around here."

That's the only information I know.

My hands falter around the dough, trembling. I even killed my own damn mother.

"What is wrong with me?" I murmur, not meaning to say it aloud.

"Hey." Izzy pats my hand with an affectionate expression. "It wasn't your fault. No one's birth is wrong."

I smile a little. Considering my bitchy nature, I doubt I was ever good to Izzy, so I'm beyond thankful she's trying to cheer me on.

"What about Alex's wife?"

Her features fall and she seems in deep thought, as if choosing her words carefully. "She died in an accident when Asher was about ten."

Oh.

On some level, Asher and I share a tragedy. The only difference is, I didn't know my mother, while he did.

Wait…

If I've never met my mother, how come I keep having these bursts of memories about her? She used to tell me things, and I remember them.

"Asher and Arianna were devastated."

"Who's Arianna?"

Izzy freezes as if she realized what she uttered is taboo. "Uh…forget about it."

"No, tell me. Please?" I soften my expression. "I feel so lost already. Don't hide other things from me."

"Asher's younger sister. One year younger, to be exact."

I didn't know Asher has a sister. There are no pictures or photo albums in this house.

"How come I've never met her?" I smile a little. "Does she also go to school abroad?

Her brows furrow as she closes the oven. "She…she passed away."

My heart thunders in my throat and nausea assaults me. Asher lost a sister? "How? When?"

She opens her mouth to reply but then commotion barges into the kitchen. Asher, Sebastian, and Owen enter, in the middle of an animated conversation.

Asher and Sebastian smile at something Owen says.

I dig my fingers into the dough as my gaze gets lost in Asher's face. The ease behind his features—it's the type of smile he never shows me.

All I get are glares and the silent treatment.

Sure enough, when his eyes land on mine, his smile falls, replaced by a calculating streak.

I try not to think about how I look. Flour covers my hands and some of my face as I stand behind the counter, wearing an apron.

"Is this the apocalypse?" Owen slides onto a stool in front of me. "Are you…"

"Baking?" Sebastian finishes for him as he snatches a cookie from the plate. He smells it as if making sure it's not plastic.

My attention remains on Asher. While Owen and Sebastian sit, flipping the cookies and goofing around, he stands there with a hand in his pocket.

His face is neutral, but I see something more now. I see someone who lost a sibling. For some reason, that type of loss rattles me more than it should.

I'm an only child so I shouldn't feel the loss of a sibling, but somehow, I do.

I open my mouth even though I don't even know what I want to tell him. I just want to say something...anything.

He swats Owen's hand, making him drop the cookie before it's halfway to his mouth.

"Dude! I was eating that."

"I just saved your life." Asher throws a menacing look my way. "It's probably poisoned."

"Ouch," Sebastian drawls, eyes twinkling. "What's it gonna be, Barbie?"

"What?" I smile to hide how much Asher's words jab at me.

"The new dare, of course." He waggles his brows. "Whose miserable soul are you going to slice and dice this time?"

"No one's." I wipe my hands on the apron more aggressively than necessary.

"Bored already?" Owen asks with a raised brow.

I level the wide receiver with a glare. "Or all of this is stupid?"

"Stupid?" Owen repeats. "You invented it, Rei-Rei."

"You could've stopped me." I meet their gazes before focusing back on Sebastian. "And you're such a hypocrite, Bastian."

He raises a hand, expression playful. "Don't put your mistakes on me."

"You could've said no instead of ruining Naomi's life."

"Ooh, someone's in the know." Owen crunches on a cookie, and for some reason, I feel grateful that he didn't listen to Asher.

Sebastian cocks his head. "Maybe I did want to ruin her life."

"Maybe you're an asshole."

"Maybe you're an entitled bitch."

"Enough." Asher stares at his friend then at me with an unreadable expression.

"Screw you all." I ignore them and head to the stairs.

"They taste awesome, Rei-Rei," Owen shouts behind me.

"Un-screw you, Owen." I smile without turning around.

He barks out a laugh. "Pretty sure that's not even a word."

"It is now."

I hear him cough as if someone elbowed him. "What? She's cool."

Before I round the corner, I steal a look behind me. Asher's gaze digs daggers into my back. His head is tilted to the side like he can't figure me out.

Good.

It's impossible to figure him out, too.

But after what Izzy told me, I'm starting to think maybe, just maybe, his hatred has to do with something I've done.

CHAPTER 18 - REINA

LIFE GOES ON...TO an extent.

The following week at college is less hectic than the previous one.

It's almost...normal, or at least what can be called normal for someone who remembers nothing about her life.

My memories are still stuck playing hide and seek.

I asked Alex if I could move back to my apartment downtown. It's not that I hate the company. I really like Izzy and Jason and the Scrabble nights we've had together.

However, I thought going back to the place I lived in for three years might bring back some of my memories.

And yes, I might've wanted to escape Asher. I've

been feeling like shit after finding out about his sister's death and that I cheated on him.

Not that he didn't likely fuck countless girls in England, but still. I hate having the cheater tag on me.

It's such a disturbing, ugly place to be.

Alex, however, denied my request. He diplomatically refused, saying there's still danger on my safety from that break-in and that I need further rest.

Later that day, I found out from Izzy we had a visit from Detective Daniels. He demanded to speak to me or have me volunteer for questioning. Alex shooed him away, threatening to file a restraining order if he comes to trouble me again.

According to Izzy, I'm lucky to have Alex with me, not against me. Apparently, he's a notoriously ruthless lawyer.

Maybe it's because of that I'm not so scared about the mafia threat. It might also have to do with the fact that the black van didn't show up again.

I sit in Lucy's car as she drives toward campus. Her purple MINI Cooper stands out in the parking lot like a cute balloon.

I have a white Lexus back at home, but I'm not confident enough to drive it yet.

Bree has been salty because I chose Lucy to be my

ride instead of her. Truth be told, I'm more comfortable with Lucy's non-bitchy character.

True, I was a worse bitch than Bree, but that Reina is gone and will never return.

The first step of redemption: not surrounding myself with demons from my past.

As we exit her car, Lucy shows me an Instagram picture of a few football players drinking in secret. It's on some account called blackwood-black-book.

"Who's awful enough to post those pictures?" I ask. "Won't that ruin their chances to be drafted into the NFL?"

"Could be." Lucy raises her shoulders. "Blackwood Black Book is all about scandal, though."

And it seems to be working based on the thousands of followers it's gained.

"Who runs it?" I ask.

"No one knows." She laughs. "It's like a Gossip Girl of sorts."

I stop, the thought of another very suspicious account barging into my mind. I hold out my hand to Lucy. "Let me see."

After she gives me the phone, I click on the account's followers and type Cloud003. Sure enough, he's there.

Motherfucker.

This should mean he's a student at Blackwood College—or close enough. Does that mean he was the one who bound me that night? But if he were, why would he warn me afterward?

"What's wrong?" Lucy leans in to peek.

I quickly wipe the search history then return her phone. "Hey, Luce?"

She grins, her prominent cheeks lifting with the motion.

"What?" I eye her closely.

"I don't think I'll ever get used to you calling me Luce." She walks beside me. "What is it?"

I clear my throat. "We've been on the same squad for three years, and you even know me from high school, right?"

"Right."

"During all that time, did I ever talk about...I don't know, a love interest or something like that?"

She hums, tapping her chin. "You never talk about your love interests."

"Not even about Asher?"

"No." She doesn't even stop to think about it. "You're a private person, Reina. None of us actually knows what goes on in your life, except for maybe Bree."

Well, shit. I had hoped it wouldn't come down to

talking to her, but I probably have to bite the bullet and do it. If she has any idea about this Cloud003 asshole, I need to know.

Still, there's something else I have to confirm with Lucy.

"Did Asher come back during Halloween parties?" I ask carefully. There's a slight chance he's Cloud003.

"Two years ago, yes. Last year, no."

"He could've come over without you seeing him." From what I understand, I always met this Cloud003 person in disguise.

"He celebrated Halloween with his friends in England last year. Hang on." She retrieves her phone and scrolls through someone's Instagram. Then she shows me a picture of Asher wrapping an arm around a guy with intimidating gray eyes. A blonde girl snuggles in his lap. Three other guys and girls stand behind them, some smiling and others in Halloween costumes.

Sure enough, the date of the picture is the night before Halloween. The caption reads, 'Remember kids, no Halloween is scarier than real people.'

Interesting.

"Whose account is this?" I ask Lucy.

She taps the face of the guy with gray eyes. "Aiden King. He's like Asher's closest friend in England. He's so dreamy. Not that I'm stalking him or anything." She sighs. "Pity he's married. I swear all the good ones are."

I wonder why he got married so young.

But anyway, this picture erases the slight suspicion that Asher is Cloud003.

A petite figure brushes past us like a wrecking ball.

"Move, Queen Bitch and follower." Naomi throws her usual remark at me.

Lucy stops talking abruptly, her mouth hanging at an awkward angle.

I step in front of Naomi, blocking her path. "That's enough."

With our height difference, she has to look up at me, but that doesn't erase the malice in her rich brown eyes. "What? No fake apologies this time?"

"If you thought that apology was fake then suit yourself, Naomi." I cross my arms over my chest. "As much as you like calling us bitches, you're no different. Lucy has done nothing wrong and doesn't deserve all these attacks."

"It's okay." Lucy touches my arm, bowing her head.

"It's not." I push her in front of Naomi. "If you were Lucy's best friend, you would know how much your treatment hurts her."

"What do you know about hurt?" Naomi's voice is calm considering the seething expression on her face.

"What do you know about suffering when you're all high and mighty?"

"Just stop, Nao," Lucy pleads, voice choking. "This isn't you."

"Yes, it is. You were just too busy following orders to notice it."

A black Tesla stops right beside us with a screech. Naomi tenses and attempts to dash toward campus. The driver's door opens, blocking her escape route.

Sebastian steps out, looking dashing in his football jacket, a messenger bag slung over his shoulders.

"Move out of the way, asshole." She tries to bypass him but doesn't raise her head.

"Was that a bee buzzing?" He strains his neck with mockery, not looking at her either.

"Move before I sting you." Her face heats with exertion.

"That would involve you getting near me, and we both know that's not going to happen, tsundere."

Naomi's face reddens. I can feel her rage coming off in waves. Her mouth opens and closes as if she wants to say something, but no words come out.

"Stop it." I pull Sebastian by the sleeve of his jacket.

Naomi takes the chance to jog toward the school building.

"You can run but you can't hide, tsundere," he calls after her.

"What does that mean?" I ask him.

He stares down at me as if just noticing my existence. "Since when do you care?"

Ugh. Okay, I get it. I was an uncaring, selfish little shit. But come on, why can't everyone stop shoving it in my face? I'm really trying here.

"Reina has changed." Lucy steps beside me, puffing her chest forward.

Thank you, Santa, for sending me a gift wrapped in the form of Lucy. Oh, and screw you, Old Reina, for not appreciating this girl.

Sebastian watches me in that suspicious way that's become everyone's MO around me.

The intrusiveness of his gaze reminds me of Asher and the death glares he's been giving me lately.

No matter how much I try to avoid his existence, a part of me always gravitates toward him.

"Prove it," Sebastian says firmly.

"Prove what?" I ask.

"That you've changed."

I'm tempted to flip him off, but that's not how redemption works. The best way to prove oneself is to give, not take, which means I have to focus on Sebastian's weaknesses and make them better.

My mind works around what I've learned about Sebastian so far—which isn't much. Since he's Asher's friend, getting close to him means circulating in Asher's orbit.

No, thanks.

But, oh well—if what I have in my mind works then it's worth a shot.

I raise an eyebrow. "You're failing psychology."

"What does that have to do with proving you've changed?"

"If you fail this semester, the coach will bench you and you might lose your chance to go pro."

His jaw works. "If there's a point behind all this, you should reach it now."

"I will help you nail psychology."

Not only am I the captain of the cheerleading team, but I'm also a straight-A student. Studying makes way more sense to me than the black and white cheerleading uniform I still haven't mustered the courage to wear.

"You lost your memory," he argues.

"I still got a perfect score on the practice test last week." I lift my shoulder. "I guess genius can't be wiped away, huh?"

Lucy smiles, shouting, "Hell yeah! She's an amazing tutor, by the way. She helped me ace Debate the other day."

"Thank you." I face Sebastian. "So what's it gonna be? My offer has an expiration date in about..." I stare at my watch. "Ten seconds. Nine, eight, seven—"

"Fine. Jesus, it's like you had a personality transplant."

"I'll take that as a compliment."

Lucy, Sebastian, and I part ways inside since we have different classes.

I say good morning to anyone who greets me, and much to my dismay, it still shocks some students, as if something holy has landed in town.

My next class is Sociology. When I walk in, no one is inside. It's only empty chairs and a screen. I turn around, searching for any human presence.

Was it canceled?

I really need to start checking the college's website more frequently.

"Is anyone here?" When no one replies, I head for the exit.

The door hisses shut in my face. I try the intercom, but there's no response.

What the hell?

I grip the handle and pull. Nothing. It's like it's made of steel.

"Come on, open—"

The lights go out. The entire room gets swallowed in punishing darkness.

My heartbeat picks up as I lose an essential sense —sight.

"Hello?" I hate how my voice trembles on the word. "This isn't funny."

I thrust my hand into my bag, fishing for my phone.

A bang sounds on the wall.

I flinch and my phone drops to the ground. The unmistakable crack of the screen echoes in the air.

"Shit." I crouch, my hands feeling around blindly.

Light bursts into the projector like an old movie. It shines onto the opposite wall.

I gasp, freezing in my crouched position.

Black words in a bloody font flash on the white walls. They pass so fast as if planning to give me epilepsy. I'm about to close my eyes when the words start registering.

I. Am. Coming. For. You. I. Know. What. You. Did. Blood. On. Your. Hands. Murderer. Murderer. MURDERER.

I cover my mouth with both of my hands as the words repeat on a loop.

No.

This is some sort of a sick joke.

I stumble backward, my heel catching on the

ground. I nearly fall, but I pull myself together and slam my palms on the door.

"Help!" I scream at the top of my lungs. "Someone help!"

I hit the door harder and faster until my palms sting and tears well in my eyes.

A ping sounds from near the projector.

I jerk, my hands turning sweaty. Perspiration slides down my temples and my neck and all the way underneath my clothes.

The lights continue flashing and flashing and fucking flashing.

I place both hands on my ears and slide to the floor.

"No, Mommy, no...don't go..." A sob tears from my throat. "Mom...Rei..."

Darkness grips me by the throat before they can come for me.

CHAPTER 19 - G

THERE'S nothing more beautiful than seeing her fall.

You know that moment when human beings lose all hope? When doors slam in their face and they just…drop?

That's what Reina does. Even her fall is graceful. She fought, I give her that. She screamed and wailed. She cried and kicked.

But no amount of tears will get her out of my mind.

She's already trapped. She's already done for.

I stand above her unmoving body. She fainted on the ground, eyes screwed shut and some of her mascara smearing over her pale cheeks. Both her hands still cover her ears as if she can stop the voices from barging in.

I crouch beside her and stroke a blonde strand

behind her ear. Her lower lip twitches and I give in to the urge to touch those lips, to run my thumb along them.

They're soft, full, and begging for my dick between them.

As if reading my mind, they slightly part. I groan deep in my throat.

Sex appeal.

Something Reina has in spades and uses to her advantage every chance she gets. I thought I was immune, but I'm not.

Because right now, I want to strip her bare and fuck her raw.

She's getting under my skin again. She can't get under my fucking skin.

I place a hand over her closed eyes and the other over her nose and mouth, cutting off her breathing.

Her lifeline.

The only things keeping her in this world.

This could end now.

Everything will be over. I'll get what I want and she'll get what she deserves.

Her slender body bucks off the floor due to the lack of oxygen. Her nails claw at my arms and her legs kick with the ferocity of life.

As much as she sometimes hates this life, she sure as fuck fights for it.

She's a fighter, Reina. A survivor—but that won't last for long.

Kill her.

Now.

I close my eyes and slowly remove my hand from over her mouth. Her gasp for air is choked and unrestrained, as if she's been dying and is now coming up for air.

She doesn't deserve such an easy death.

Not yet.

Her body slumps back down and her arms fall on either side of her.

A commotion comes from the other side of the door.

I stand up and memorize her broken form, committing it to memory.

"It'll all be over soon," I say. "It'll all be over."

IT'LL all be over soon, a sinister voice calls above me. *It'll all be over.*

I jolt awake, gasping for air as if I'm being resurrected.

The dark space disappears and buildings sprint past me. Am I in a…car?

My head snaps to the side, expecting to find whoever trapped me in class. He put his hand on my face. He suffocated me. He…wanted to kill me.

Oh, God.

All I remember is a blurry black silhouette as he walked away, but I would know him if I saw him.

He's engraved in my subconscious like an enormous crow, a larger-than-life Grim Reaper.

My breathing comes down a notch when I make out the driver's face.

Asher.

He drives with one hand on the wheel, his attention on the road.

It's mind-boggling how much his presence calms me down. This shouldn't be, right? Asher isn't my safe space.

He *can't* be.

I stare down at my jeans and camisole. They look intact. I should be fine...right?

Tingles push to my nose and pressure builds behind my eyes, but I hold in the tears...the humiliation, the pain.

When the hell will I stop my life from getting away from me? It just keeps slipping from between my fingers like water.

Realizing I'm awake, Asher throws a glance my way, or more like a stare. He has this thing about digging into my soul with those forest green eyes. It's like he's dissecting my insides and dancing on the remains.

He smoothly focuses back on the road. "What happened?"

"What am I doing here, Ash?"

He grinds his teeth. "It's Asher. And answer my

question."

"Answer mine first."

He gives me a fleeting glance. "I picked you up."

I picked you up.

He makes it sound so easy, as if I wasn't dying in there.

"What happened, Reina?" he repeats in a less patient tone.

"I went to class and..." My fight with tears turns intense. I can feel myself losing to the pull. "Someone trapped me. I...I..."

"You fainted?" he finished for me.

I shake my head. That's not what happened. I had a flashback, but none of it makes sense now. It's like an old, fuzzy, gray movie with white and black dots.

"You found me?" I peek at him through my wet eyelashes. There's a sick type of gratefulness for this man whirling inside me.

A shiver runs down my spine at the thought of what could've happened.

Asher is a jerk, but he's a jerk who saved me.

"Lucy called me," he says with ease. "You're not important enough for me to notice your absence."

I pause my imaginary thank-you dance, and my fingers twitch for something stabby—preferably a knife straight to his throat.

Why the hell does he have to ruin my image of him? Every time I get close, he becomes an asshole and ruins it.

"Sorry to have ruined your plans." I stare out the window.

"It was nothing important, just coffee with Brianna."

My body tightens until I'm sure some muscle or tendon will pop. I didn't know Asher and Bree were close enough to have coffee without me.

Coffee.

It's an excuse husbands give their wives when they're cheating on them.

Breathe, Reina. You don't care about this asshole.

He and Bree can get married and have demonic babies for all I care. But if they think they can play me for a fool, they have another thing coming.

I open my mouth to roast him alive but immediately close it. What right do I have when I've cheated on him first?

This is that karma thing, isn't it?

For a long minute, silence stretches between us like a third passenger. Asher drives with his usual poker face while I seethe on the inside.

Volcanoes and hurricanes are running rampant in my head. I want payback, but I know if I act rashly, if I blindly give in to my emotions, the whole thing will flip against me.

"Do they know who trapped me in there?" I ask with a cool voice.

"You have too many enemies to count." He announces it like it's the weather forecast—a given, a normalcy.

"Starting with you."

His piercing eyes hold mine hostage. "Starting with me."

"If you hate me so much, why are you driving me home?"

"Image and all that." He pauses. "I couldn't stand there while the entire college saw you at your lowest."

I gulp and fumble for my bag. I find the phone inside; the screen is fractured like my breathing.

It doesn't take me long to figure out what Asher means. On the blackwood-black-book IG account, there's a picture of me sprawled out on the classroom's floor with my mascara streaked and my hands covering my ears. My hair camouflages half of my face, but it's obvious that it's me.

There's no caption. As usual with BBB's pictures, it's just hashtags.

#FallOfAQueen #Look #SheCanCry

The picture has over a thousand likes and a few

hundred comments.

'Did someone play a prank on her?'

'Is this a joke?'

'I heard she's been crazy since she disappeared.'

'I swear I saw Jason, the Knights' quarterback, drop her off. Knights' whore.'

I close my eyes and power off the phone. I don't know what stings more—the picture, the number of people taking pleasure in my fall, or maybe the asshole who had coffee with Bree while I was living a nightmare.

Pressure builds behind my eyes all over again.

Since I returned, I've been trying my hardest to atone and make amends, but nothing is working. No one likes me in that goddamn college no matter what I do.

"Aww, are you going to cry?" Asher mocks, a cruel edge in his voice.

I wipe at the blurriness in my eyes and stare out the window, ignoring him.

He won't see me break.

He won't see me cry.

"By all means, don't stop on my account, my ugly monster."

"You think all this is fun and games?" I face him and fold my arms over my chest.

He does that staring thing again. His attention is like a living breathing thing, sharp and cutting.

I hate how gorgeous he looks in his simple white shirt. The sleeves are rolled to his elbows, revealing taut forearms.

And the veins.

Jeez. His strong veins disappear underneath the shirt along with the tattoo I know is in there. His hair is combed today, but he still gives off 'fuck the world' vibes.

"I don't know." He taps his finger on the steering wheel ever so casually. "You tell me."

"I thought I was dying." My voice rises with pent-up frustration. "I could've died in there!"

"And yet you didn't." His cold, unfeeling tone cuts me so deep I'm surprised there's not blood all over the expensive leather of his car.

"Is that what you want?" I murmur. "Would it make you happy if I died?"

He shakes his head once as he pulls into the house's driveway. "You give yourself so much credit. Your life or death means shit to me, monster."

"Stop calling me that! I'm not a monster. I am *not*." My voice breaks along with my heart.

He saved me. *Twice.*

Surely that means something. Surely he can't be

such a stone.

Asher hits the brakes so hard, I jerk forward, but the seat belt holds me in place.

Before I can make out what's going on, he lunges out of the car, strides to my side, and yanks me out of the seat as if I were a rag doll.

He lifts me up and carries me bridal style with ease, strolling into the mansion just like that first time he walked me to my room.

My breast brushes against his shirt and my jeans are the only barrier between my skin and his steel-like hand.

For a moment, I'm too stunned to react. For a moment, I get lost in the contact of our bodies, the tightening of my nipples, the torturous friction and the aching sensation.

I shake my head, the stupefaction withering away.

My hands turn into fists and I hit him. "What are you doing? Let me down."

He continues as if he doesn't feel my punches.

One or two of the staff poke their heads out but quickly hide once Asher throws them a glance—or more like a glare.

Blood rushes to my cheeks at the scene they must be seeing. I can't believe this is happening.

He takes the steps two at a time and barges into my

room like a bull. I expect him to throw me on the bed like the other time and play some intimidation game with me, but he goes straight to the bathroom.

I don't get a warning before he drops me inside the shower and turns the water on.

It drenches me in a second. Cold. Freezing.

I shriek, my clothes and hair getting soaked and sticking to my skin. I gurgle as the strong flow hits me in the nose and mouth, cutting off my air supply.

Choking on my open breaths, I trip and slip backward. He grabs my arm in a painful grip, his skin ice cold on mine. He tugs me forward, I fall to my knees, and his onslaught continues.

"S-st...op..." I gasp, fighting for air.

The water comes out of my nose and my mouth at the same time.

"Stop?" He laughs with enough menace to make chills erupt all over my skin. "You're only tasting your own medicine, Reina. You claim you're not a monster, but how about that dare in high school? Do you know what you did back then? You dared a second year to hose a freshman in the boys' locker room. He had fucking asthma and almost died. You're lucky you don't have asthma. You can survive a little breath play, can't you, my ugly monster?"

Tears spring to my eyes, mixing with the water. My

heart tightens, suffocating with my lungs.

"Come out," he challenges, as if I'm a bet he's trying to win. "Show me your ugly face—your *only* face. Stop pretending you're a saint when the devil runs in your veins."

I flail my arms around, trying to protect my face.

It doesn't work.

For a second, I feel like I'll die. I can't face death twice in one day and come out victorious.

He cuts off the water. I gasp on air, panting and choking on my own breaths.

Oxygen burns the more I gulp it in.

"Are you going to stop this nice-person game?" His voice is so low it's threatening.

"I…I'm n-not…pretending. I've changed." The old Reina isn't me anymore.

Water splashes my face again. "Wrong answer."

I gurgle on unsaid words as I gasp and fail to breathe.

God. I think my lungs will bail on me.

"We'll try again. When I turn off the water, I want you to…" He trails off. "No. You love dares, so let's do it your way. I *dare* you to be who you truly are."

The water stops. I gasp in as much air as I can, knowing it probably won't last me for long before he asphyxiates me again.

With all the defiance I can muster, I stare him in the eyeballs. "This is me, the only *me*. If you're too afraid to accept that then fuck you, Ash."

His hold on the knob falters for a brief second before he points the showerhead in my direction again.

I take one last breath, bracing myself for the hit, but I don't close my eyes. I'm going to glare at him as he does it.

I'm going to look straight into his empty soul and make sure he sees my fight.

Reina Ellis wasn't born to be trampled on.

Instead of drowning me, he steps away.

"I promise you one thing. You will break." The coldness of his eyes nearly freezes me.

But it doesn't.

I don't let it.

I jut out my chin. "Never."

His eyes twinkle with something unreadable before he turns around and leaves.

I slump to the floor, all soaked as I catch my breath.

In this moment, I dare to make a promise to myself.

College and gossip won't break me.

Whoever trapped me won't break me.

No one will.

Asher included.

CHAPTER 21 - REINA

"IGNORE THEM, REINA." Lucy rubs the side of my arm as if that will make the goosebumps go away.

Everyone in the cafeteria is staring at us. Or rather, they're staring at me. Since that incident two days ago, I've been called every name possible.

People are starting to take pictures of my every move and sending them to that shady Instagram account.

I hate that I subconsciously search all around me as if expecting someone to jump at me.

It's like everyone waited for this moment to roast me. Even those who remain silent are secretly appreciating my fall from grace.

"Let's sit with the football team?" Lucy prompts with a beaming smile.

At the far end of the cafeteria, the football team and some of the cheerleading squad sit together—Bree included.

Of course, Asher is with his jerk friends.

Everyone laughs and plays around. Not him. His entire attention is on me as if he's been watching me since I walked in.

It's a thing he does, watching me without being obvious, like I'm the center of his focus. The pent-up energy hangs between us like a threat, irrational and unchained.

It's stupid, isn't it? I'm not supposed to feel a connection with an asshole who's out to ruin my life.

I'm not supposed to watch him watch me at breakfast with Izzy or when he's working out in the backyard.

I'm not supposed to stay up late just to see him return and stand by his car for a second too long, staring up at my window as if searching for something.

Or someone.

Now, our gazes clash and collide. Mine is defiant and unbending, his is challenging and quiet.

I can't help the shivers bursting down my spine or the heat invading the tiniest pores of my skin.

Staring at Asher is beyond gazes and eyes. It's a

war with weapons, blood, and casualties. It's impossible to predict who'll lose and who'll win.

One thing's for certain: I'll never raise the white flag.

I'll pick my battles instead.

Breaking eye contact, I make a beeline toward a back table where the rest of the cheerleaders sit. 'The less popular ones,' as Bree so eloquently put it.

I smile when joy breaks out on the girls' faces. I hate that the others put them down and that I never cared to see happiness on their faces before.

Lucy slides in beside me, shaking her head. "You do know you can't avoid the main table forever, right?"

"I'm not avoiding it. I just don't want to sit with them." I take a bite of my pizza and chew slowly.

Screw salads. So what if I don't get thrown in the air anymore? It's not like I've been dying to return to that 'epic' position.

"Are you coming back to the captain position?" Cindy, a sophomore, asks with a timid voice.

"I don't know." And I really don't. Cheerleading isn't my goal in life. True, I'm still not sure what my actual goal *is*, but cheerleading is definitely not it.

Besides, this is senior year. They'll have to elect a new captain soon. Doing it at the beginning or the end of the year shouldn't make a difference.

My gaze strays to the 'main' table. Bree sits on Asher's right, running her red-manicured fingers along his bicep…his strong, veiny bicep. She giggles at something he says like some silly teenager with a crush.

He's eating while throwing glances her way.

Something boils in my bloodstream, turning it all hot and green.

How can Bree, who claims I'm her best friend, flirt with my fiancé right in front of me?

Not that I want to sit next to Asher. *Ever.*

But still, I don't like people stepping all over me, especially fake friends like Bree.

"At this rate, there will be a division in the squad." There's a sadness in Lucy's voice as she plays with a fork on her salad plate.

"Correction." Naomi slams her plate down and sits across from me. She usually doesn't even eat in the cafeteria. "Lucy is too nice to tell you there's already a division in the squad." Naomi points at the cheerleaders, the boys and girls sitting with Bree. "Bitch Uno's Team." She motions at our table. "Bitch Dos' Team."

The girls gasp, but Naomi isn't done. She takes a bite of her pizza and speaks casually. "I wonder who will win. Actually, scratch that—you're losing by forfeiting."

"Stop it, Nao," Lucy scolds.

"Nah, your captain seems to have buried her head in the sand like Little Miss Ostrich, so it's time for a wake-up call." Naomi throws her hands around. "Bree has been all over Asher like a snake and you're letting her. She's taking over the squad and you're letting her. She's snatching your position at this college and—OMG, shocker—you're letting her. Hashtag fall of a queen."

I suck in a long breath. "Have you ever thought maybe I don't want to be on those pedestals anymore?"

Naomi laughs. "Could've fooled me."

"I'm not joking, and I don't have to prove myself to you or to anyone else." I put down my pizza. "I'm done being the old Reina. I won't go out of my way to be someone I'm not."

Silence falls over the table as if I've spoken holy words.

"So…what?" Naomi narrows her eyes. "You fell once and now you're abdicating the throne?"

I smile. "I don't remember having any throne to abdicate. I lost my memories."

"But we didn't. None of us did." The maliciousness in Naomi's voice takes me by surprise.

"Nao…" Lucy trails off.

"No." She shakes her head. "Memories on or off, you're still a selfish bitch, Reina."

"What is that supposed to mean?" My tone hardens.

"You're leaving it all to Bree knowing exactly the type of freak she is. All you care about is getting yourself out of the spotlight."

"Why do you care? Don't you hate me?"

"I do, but the other girls look up to you for some reason. The least you can do is protect them from Bree's fat-shaming remarks and dictatorship. Did you know she makes the less pretty ones go on insane diets and do individual workouts until they almost pass out from hunger and exhaustion? Did you know she's having them do the male cheerleaders' work? Of course you don't. As I said, you only care about yourself."

"Is that true?" I ask the girls.

Lucy winces before she and a few other girls bow their heads with pained expressions.

Oh.

I bite my lower lip so hard I'm surprised blood doesn't come out. So this is what the others have been going through while I was hiding in my room and skipping watching them at practice.

While I was too engrossed in myself, the girls have been at Bree's mercy—or lack thereof.

Old Reina might not have done much for these girls before, but that will change now.

I won't sit back and watch as they're being mistreated.

Straightening my spine, I meet Naomi's gaze. "I'll step up under one condition."

She gives me a quizzical glance but says nothing.

"You need to forgive me, Naomi."

Soft gasps echo from the girls as they watch us closely.

Her lips purse. "Why is that important?"

"It is to me." My voice softens. "Don't you want to protect the girls?"

"Why would you think I want to do that?" She maintains her signature glare, but I know she cares deep down or she wouldn't have asked me to help them.

"Come on," Lucy pleads.

"I need allies," I coax.

"You must be out of your mind if you think you'll have that in me." Naomi flicks her silky black hair back. "I'm your enemy, Reina."

"Well, you know what they say about keeping your enemies closer than your friends."

"You've become such a freaking weirdo." She rises to her feet. "So, are we doing this or what?"

I smile as I stand up with both Lucy and Naomi on either side of me. The rest of the girls and some boys follow suit, one by one.

"Let's go get my place back," I say with all my confidence.

Naomi leans in to whisper, "I'll gut you if you return to your old bitchy self."

I smirk. "Is that a promise?"

She shakes her head. "That blunt-force trauma really did a number on you."

We stride toward the main table. Everyone in the cafeteria watches us closely, seeming to hold their breath.

Silence fills the space as everyone at the main table stops talking all at once.

I stand there, carrying my plate, straightening my shoulders.

Prescott offers an awkward smile. "Hey, Captain."

Bree reprimands him with a look and presses her lips into a thin line.

Owen jumps up from his seat and grins at us. "Long time no see, Rei-Rei. Are you here for that offer?"

"I'm here for my place." I meet Bree's stare head-on. She has enough decency to stop rubbing her hand along Asher's arm, but she doesn't let him go.

I refuse to look him in the eye even though I feel him boring holes in my face. One look, one freaking glance and all the courage I've summoned might evaporate.

"Oh, what to do?" Bree asks with a honeyed voice. "The table doesn't fit everyone."

I lean over, plant my hand in front of her, and mimic her fake smile. "Then I guess you have to make room for the captain."

Everyone at the table—and the entire cafeteria—grows silent, seemingly entranced by the duel.

This will either bury her or bury me.

And I haven't returned from the dead to be buried.

"It's okay!" Lucy rushes in. "I'm sure we can attach an extra table."

"Hear that, Bree?" I tell her. "Go fetch the table."

She doesn't move, her face growing red with exertion. "Reina, you—"

I slam my tray in front of hers, shutting her up. I lean forward and snarl, "*Move.*"

Her mouth falls open, but no words come out. Her ears heat, looking close to combustion. It's Prescott who grabs her by the arm.

I remove her hand from Asher's arm and plant my ass right beside him.

"Right, ladies." Owen chuckles. "We'll help with the table."

A few other guys from the team laugh along with him and go to fetch one. Naomi smiles in my peripheral vision, and I can't help but smile back.

No one will step on me.

So what if I was a terrible person in the past? I'm changing, and no one will make me feel bad about that.

A heavy arm slings over my shoulder. I breathe in his sandalwood and citrus scent as I focus on his touch surrounding me.

Asher's hot breath tickles my ear. "What are you doing?"

I swallow, squashing the flutters in my chest and the tightening of my belly. The flaw in this plan? Having to be this close to Asher.

It's becoming harder and harder to control my reaction around him. A part of me sees him as the one who breathes life into me, the one who saved me twice.

And it's a wrong thought to have about someone who means me no good.

"It has nothing to do with you," I murmur back.

Down, body. Stay the hell down.

His lips graze the shell of my ear. A whimper gets trapped in my throat as he bites down for a split second.

"Is that so?" The rumble of his voice awakens goosebumps on my skin.

How can he pack so much sexual energy in three mere words?

My body catches fire from his lips and voice on my

ear. I squirm in my seat, fighting to not make a sound or lean into his touch.

"What if I want it to be about me?" His voice deepens with darkness so tangible I taste it on my tongue.

My head snaps in his direction. He watches me closely, but it's not intimidation. It's almost like…he's seeing me in a different light.

A new light.

A brighter light.

"Didn't you…" My voice catches and I clear my throat. "Didn't you say you don't want anything to do with me?"

"You keep barging in anyway." He licks the shell of my ear one more time. "It's time I trap you."

I GLIDE the pen against my lower lip and bite down on it. I sit at the pool, a notepad on my legs, but I'm not studying.

My gaze keeps flitting to the backyard—or, more specifically, to the sleek, cut abdomen and back. They glisten with sweat as Asher switches from short runs to push-ups.

I mean, the least he can do is wear a damn T-shirt. But no, he always works out in just shorts as if he's offended by anything on top.

It's not that my eyes are complaining, but there's a tiny little problem with my body becoming hot and bothered by the view.

The simplest solution would be to stop watching, but for the life of me, I can't keep my eyes off him.

He's like a magnet and I'm helpless steel. He's the fire and I'm the moth waiting to be burned.

I wish this weird infatuation were because of that tousled hair sticking to his forehead, the six-pack cut to perfection, the broad shoulders, or the intricate tattoo rippling up his bicep.

I wish it were all about the unfairly handsome face or the 'fuck you' aura he exudes so well. I really wish the tugging and pulling at the bottom of my stomach were only because I'm drawn to his exterior charm.

But that's not, is it?

Something wild and crazy lurks under the surface between us. This twisted connection started that first day in the hospital, and it's refused to stop ever since.

Like a current of water, the harder I fight it, the stronger it pulls me under.

My phone pings, and I nearly drop my pen. Shifting to face forward, I check my messages.

It's my group chat with Lucy and Naomi.

Lucy: Let's meet. Reina? Nao?
Naomi: Fine, but don't you dare go sappy on me.

I grin as I type.

Reina: Sappy is my middle name, dude.

Luce sends a laughing emoji, and Naomi sends a GIF of a girl rolling her eyes.

They're seriously the only two I find comfort with. Despite her tough act, Naomi cares and is very mushy inside. Lucy is just Lucy, nice and supportive even if it affects her own comfort.

A notification from Instagram appears on my screen.

It's a message. Cloud003.

My smile falls and my heart rate picks up. I can hear the roaring in my ears as I click on it.

Cloud003: I've been thinking a lot about your lips around my dick lately.
Cloud003: Or your pussy. I'm not picky.

My cheeks heat as I watch my surroundings. Asher is running in the distance, his back rippling, and no one else is around.

Reina-Ellis: Screw off or I'll report this to the police.
Cloud003: The same police who are investigating you for murder?

How the hell does he know that?

Cloud003: Admit it, my slut. You want my cock as much as it wants you.

Reina-Ellis: Whatever happened between us is over. Move the fuck on.

The only one I can think about in a sexual way is the one running in the distance with earbuds in.

This mysterious asshole on Instagram does nothing for me. Old Reina was weird like that.

Cloud003: We'll see about that.

I exit Instagram altogether and lift my head. Jason heads toward me, smirking at his phone.

When his dark eyes meet mine, he slips it in his jacket and loses the smirk.

I glance at my phone then back at him.

That…can't be possible. Jason isn't Cloud003.

He can't be.

"Hey, Princess." He smiles down at my sitting position near the pool.

We've been studying together for a few weeks now. I help him out with his tests. In return, Jason has been sort of like my personal trainer to help me get back in shape before I return to being thrown in the air.

"Hey, Jace." I watch him closely as if seeing him

for the first time.

The mocha skin and kind eyes, the broad football body and the easy smile.

He can't possibly be Cloud003. And yet...something nags at me to prove it.

Best way? Surprise element. If I catch him off guard, he'll have only a fraction of a second to pull himself together, and that's my moment to read him.

"Do you know the Instagram account Cloud003?" I ask nonchalantly.

He pauses, his smile faltering a little.

Oh, God, no.

This can't be happening.

The conversation I had with him before stabs me in the mind. When I asked him if we were friends, he said, 'Something like that.'

Turns out we were friends with benefits.

"No. I barely post anything there, anyway." He smiles again. "Is it someone you know?"

"Not really." I mimic his smile.

Two can play this game, asshole.

I won't show my cards unless I know his purpose. The realization nearly breaks my heart.

These past few weeks, I was getting used to having him as a friend.

He motions at the trampoline near the pool. "Are

you ready to practice your jumps?"

I tuck all the revelations to the back of my mind and focus on the present. Jason can't know I figured it out. I need to act like before.

I stare between him and the trampoline. "No?"

"Come on. Dancing and jumping were your side hustle."

That's the thing. I don't think they speak of me anymore, and I have zero confidence about my ability to do it. However, I already promised the girls, and I'll do whatever it takes to make up for the past.

So what if I fall and break my neck?

Dramatic much, Reina?

I abandon my notepad and hop up onto the trampoline.

Jason stands there with both his arms stretched out in front of him.

I start doing minor jumps I've practiced so far. It's easy on the trampoline since it pulls me back down.

I do a major jump and flip in the air then return to the trampoline.

A rush of adrenaline tightens my stomach. There's something amazing about floating in the air; those seconds are…freedom.

Maybe that's why Old Reina stuck with cheer-leading after high school.

"Now come over," Jason prompts.

I take several deep breaths, still jumping on the trampoline. I can't trust him with my life, especially after what I just unraveled.

However, if I refuse to, he'll grow suspicious.

So I close my eyes and jump in his direction, flipping in the air.

Strong arms catch me in a cage-like embrace. I squeal. "I did it!"

Wait, Jason was wearing a T-shirt—how come he's now…naked?

I open my eyes, and all words catch in my throat. The eyes looking down at me aren't Jason's brown ones; they're deep green. Like an ocean, they pull me in and push me out.

For a moment, I'm glad my heart is actually trapped by a ribcage and won't jump out of my chest.

A tremor rushes through my limbs, and I'm not sure if it's because of the adrenaline wave or the feel of Asher's arms around my waist.

He caught me.

I search for Jason. He stands by the side, rubbing the back of his neck and appearing uncomfortable.

Did Asher push him out of the way or something?

"You can go, Jason." Asher is speaking to him, but his entire attention remains on me.

Like he doesn't want to look away.

Or *can't.*

"No." I'm surprised my tone is level. "Jason and I are practicing."

"You're practicing with me now."

"Pass." I try to push off Asher, but his grip tightens around my waist until it's almost painful.

Whenever I used to talk back to Asher, he'd give me looks of suspicion or even surprise. Those have completely disappeared lately. Now, he just watches me with all these dark, heated stares that flip my stomach upside down.

"I'll just go," Jason offers, shooting an undecipherable glance at Asher before he rounds the corner.

"Put me down," I mutter, gritting my teeth.

Surprisingly, he does set me on my feet, but he doesn't remove his hand from around my waist. He's too close, my breasts colliding with his chest...his hard, naked chest that's glistening with sweat.

My senses fill with his sandalwood and citrus scent, like a warm, sunny day. The place where his hand touches me erupts with heat even though my top serves as a barrier.

My pulse picks up pace the more his attention swallows me whole. It's like he can reach inside me and flip a switch to bring me back to life.

Refusing to get sucked into his orbit, I glare full on. "What do you think you're doing?"

He motions at the trampoline. "You said you want to practice. I'll catch you."

"I was doing that just fine with Jason."

His grip tightens until I wince and his voice comes low. "Is this a new game?"

"What's the game in practicing with Jason?"

"The fact that you never hung out with him before, or that you never called him a *friend*."

"Well, I do now."

"What changed?"

"Me. I changed, Ash. I'm not the same Reina you used to know."

"Asher." His jaw ticks as if he's searching for patience. "The name is Asher."

"That's one more thing that's changed. I like Ash better."

He pauses for a second too long. I made him speechless, and my insides dance at the thought. It's so rare to make Asher Carson speechless.

His free hand trails up to my cheek and winds around my throat, but he's not squeezing. He's merely running his fingers along my skin, as if re-learning it.

Heat invades me and goosebumps form on the skin he touches.

"You've changed," he says slowly.

Finally.

"You're even blushing."

"I'm not," I yell, but even I can feel the pits of fire on my cheeks.

He runs the pad of his calloused thumb over my cheek as if to prove a point, to lure me into his trap like a predator would do to its prey.

"Is that so, Reina?"

"Stop it," I hiss, looking around. We're in view of the staff's entrance. Anyone could come out and see us.

"I wonder what I'll find if I check."

"Check what?" I breathe.

"If I reach under those little shorts, pull your panties to the side, and thrust two fingers into your pussy, what will I find?"

It's as if someone doused me with fuel, igniting a fire.

If I was blushing before then his dirty words have me all crimson now. The bottom of my stomach contracts with wicked anticipation.

Logically, I know I need to stop him, but I can't fight the need to know more, to dig more.

Just *more*.

"So? What will I find, Reina?"

The whisper of my name out of his mouth isn't just

a name. It's a promise. A damnation. A sinister journey that pulls me closer, refusing to let me go.

Who knew my damn name could have this effect?

His hand slides from my waist to the space where my shorts meet my thighs. I suck in a breath through my teeth at the feel of his fingers disappearing under the fabric.

His thumb and forefinger grip my chin as he murmurs, "Will I find you wet?"

I bite my lower lip to stop the voice that's trying to escape.

And yes, I'm totally wet. My thighs have been slick with arousal since the moment he caught me against his half-naked body.

"I guess I have to find out on my own." His hand stops between my thighs. I might have parted them, hoping for more friction or something.

Anything.

"I'm not stupid enough to think you've been saving yourself for me, but I want to know." His voice drops to a dangerous range that feeds the goosebumps on my arms.

I throw him a curious glance as I fight the symphony of feelings going through me. That's all I can do when I'm with him.

Feel.

And sometimes, like right now, it's too much. Everything is crashing down on me from every side.

"Who did you give it up to?" The lust is still there, but something a lot more frightening lurks underneath.

"W-what?"

"Your virginity, prom queen. Who took it?"

Prom queen.

It's the first time he's called me that. It's usually monster this or monster that.

I focus back on his question. Isn't he my fiancé since I was ten or something? He should have been my first, no?

I watch him closely, his broad shoulders and sculpted face, the way his body angles toward mine both in menace and in something else.

If I had this man, I wouldn't think about cheating on him.

But then again, Old Reina and I don't think the same. Maybe she wasn't as hung up on Asher as I am. In that case, we totally need to talk so she can give me pointers on how to pull myself out of his spell.

"Was it Jason?" he continues in that cool, threatening tone. "Someone on the team? Or wait…" He looks me up and down. "Did you pull a 'fuck you' card and give it to Owen or Sebastian? Maybe both at the same time?"

I pull my fist back and slam it into his chest. It's hard enough that he stumbles backward, putting much-needed space between us.

Pressure builds behind my eyes, but I refuse to let him see that.

I refuse to let him see how much he affects me.

"If you want to think of me as a slut, go ahead, but don't you dare imply I'd put myself down just to get back at you. Newsflash, Ash: you don't deserve any of my actions to be dedicated to you." I flip my hair, having learned from Naomi how much that fills me with confidence. "And you're such an asshole for thinking so little of your friends. You don't deserve Owen and Sebastian."

I turn to leave, but a strong hand clasps around my wrist and pulls me back. I end up flush against his hard, naked chest as his eyes search mine.

There's something in them that's never been there before. It's like he's really searching for something—or someone.

His perfect brows draw together over stormy eyes that dissect my soul with each passing second.

"Who the fuck are you?" he murmurs, still watching me like a hawk.

I place a hand over his chest, wanting—no, *needing* him to understand.

"I don't know, Ash. I really don't know who I am anymore. I woke up one day with no recollection of who or what I am, and I learned how much of a monster I've been. But I'm trying. I swear I'm *really* trying to be better and to make up for what I've done. So how about you help me out? If you tell me what I did to you, I'll do everything in my power to fix it."

I didn't expect anything out of my confession. Asher already has his perception about me, and it'll take a miracle to change it.

He takes me by complete surprise when he sighs as if in defeat. "Some things can't be fixed."

I soften my voice. "Try me."

"You might have lost your memories, but I didn't." His voice turns biting. "I remember *everything*. It's all I can remember."

My heart thumps loud and hard as if about to escape my chest. There's so much hate in his eyes. It's like a deadly disease eating him from the inside out. There's a bit of confusion, too, but his hateful side suffocates everything else.

A lump the size of a ball lodges at the back of my throat as I choke the words out. "What did I do? Tell me."

"You ruined my fucking life, monster." His usual

hardness disappears. His words are a cold, frosty statement that freezes me to the bone.

I open my mouth to say something then a shadow approaches us from the side. Asher releases me, and I stumble backward as if I've been burned.

"Rei." Alex stops beside us with a clipped smile on his face, the one I call his lawyer smile. He usually uses that to ward off unwanted attention, or whenever he has a conversation with Asher.

That is, when they actually do speak.

Alex and Asher might look like father and son, but their conversations are non-existent. I barely see them acknowledge each other in the house.

Either the father-son link is too invisible, or it's simply broken. Izzy once said Alex pays a shitload of money for Asher's education, but that's it.

It's sad he thinks his relationship with his son is all about money. It also scared me to think perhaps my relationship with my father wasn't any different.

"Can you come to my office?" Alex asks me.

I throw a glance at Asher in question, but he's clenching his fists and looking away.

"Why?" I ask.

"Detective Daniels is back." He grinds his molars. "This time, he has a warrant."

THE ATMOSPHERE in Alex's office couldn't be any more suffocating.

There's this smell in the air, something potent and thick. It's not the scent of the coffee in front of the detective or the scotch at the minibar.

I sit on the sofa opposite Detective Daniels, my hands resting on my knees and my pulse skyrocketing.

It doesn't help that Asher decided to join us. It's the first time I've seen him come into his father's office of his own accord.

Letting my hair camouflage my gaze, I peek at him from under my lashes. He's still in his shorts from the workout and just threw on a T-shirt. Usually, he'd be watching me back, but he's not now.

His entire attention is on the detective, as if he has a feud with him.

"What do you want from Reina, detective?" Alex asks from his position beside me with an edge of authority.

I can feel the detective's gaze on me as he speaks. "We have a warrant to bring Miss Ellis in for questioning."

"And what are the charges?" Alex presses.

"We found her bracelet at the fire site."

"As I said before, that's only circumstantial evidence that won't hold up in court—"

Detective Daniels cuts Alex off. "We also have her DNA."

Blood drains from my face, and my head snaps upright. The first thing I see is Asher's poker face.

His unreadable expression doesn't necessarily mean something good. I'm starting to think he's the type who straps his emotions tight behind a controlled mask.

No. I want to tell him. *I didn't do anything.*

"If you please, Miss Ellis," the detective says, "come with us to the station for some questions."

"Absolutely not." Alex stands. "Bring an arrest warrant for that."

"You're only making it harder for her." The detective meets my gaze, harsh and judgmental. He already thinks I had a hand in whatever happened at that cottage, and nothing will change his mind. "If you confess, we'll think about reducing the charges."

"I...I..." Words lodge in my throat like tiny needles, prickling the skin.

"Don't answer that, Reina." Alex walks to the door and opens it. "The voluntary questioning is over, detective."

Daniels stands up and slaps his notepad against his thigh. His eyes meet mine and a shudder slides down my spine. "Kids like you are a cancer to society and should be put down."

"That's enough, detective." Alex ushers him out. "Leave. *Now.*"

Tears blur my vision as I ball my fists in my lap. No matter how much I want to ignore his last words, I just can't.

What if...what if I really did something?

Old Reina was bad enough to hurt people, but she wasn't a criminal, right?

Once the detective leaves, Alex faces me with a reassuring smile. "Don't worry. He has nothing that will pull you down."

"But..." I gulp. "He said they found my DNA."

"But they still have no victim or suspect profile yet.

He's trying to intimidate you. Do *not* fall for his tactics. Okay?"

I nod slowly.

"You go rest, Reina."

I'm on autopilot as I stand up and exit his office. I don't stop to see the way Asher watches me. I don't want to witness the cruelty in his face or that 'See? You're a monster' look.

My legs barely carry me, and my shoulders hunch as if a weight is pulling them down.

The moment I arrive at my room, I sit on the edge of the bed, my unsteady leg unable to carry me anymore.

My heart flips and thumps in my chest so hard it's impossible to hear anything else. Pressure builds behind my eyes and my nose tingles with unshed tears.

God...what have I done?

I lift my head, and my blurry gaze collides with Asher's.

What...?

Did he follow me out of his father's office?

The need to stand up and hug him burns inside me, and I can't think of anything past that.

I don't know when he became this important, but he...did.

This is some sort of syndrome. It must've started after he saved my life.

He stalks toward me until he's standing above me. I look up, no idea what he sees on my face—sadness, chaos, or something else. I just hope he sees how lost I am right now.

How much I need him to not dig the knife in deeper.

He opens his mouth to say something, but I cut him off with a trembling voice.

"Stop."

If he slices me with his words right now, I'll just bleed to death.

His hand wraps around my throat. It's tight, as if he wants to suffocate the life out of me.

My lungs burn with the need for air.

My nails claw at his hands, trying to shake him off, to get some oxygen into my lungs.

"You don't deserve the life you've been given." He's angry—no, he's enraged, but strangely, it doesn't feel directed at me. It seems to be more about him.

"Ash…ugh…" No more words come out.

He's stealing my breath and my air supply.

"Give back what you owe," he snarls in my face.

It's the first time I've seen him so furious.

So manic.

So out of control.

He's shed his deadly calm exterior and is coming at me full force.

Tears stream down my cheeks, into my mouth, and onto his hands until all I taste is salt. I couldn't stop them even if I wanted to, because not only am I crying for myself, I'm crying for everyone whose life I made hell in the past.

Asher is one of them.

He's just one of them.

Second chance? I don't deserve that. People who are monsters like me simply don't deserve it.

"Fuck!" He jerks away from me as if he's been burned. "Stop crying."

A sob tears from my throat as I catch my breath, sucking as much air as possible into my starved lungs.

His fingers find my cheek and he wipes the tears away, a pained expression covering his face. "Why are you crying? Do you think you're a victim?"

I shake my head frantically. "I'm crying because I recognize I've been the villain all along."

His expression tightens and so does his jaw. "Why do you keep saying shit like that?"

"Like what?"

"Like you care. Like you *feel*."

"I do feel. So much, it's suffocating."

Something inside unlocks. A deep longing for him, his forgiveness, and his…everything.

I might not be able to fix all I've done in the past, but I don't want Asher mad at me. He's been mad for so long.

I hurt him for so long, and I want to fix that.

His T-shirt sticks to his stiff chest and shoulder muscles like a second skin. I want to relieve that stiffness.

To loosen him up.

I don't allow myself to think twice as I fall to my knees in front of him. I taste his sandalwood scent on my tongue and feel it seep into every pore of my skin.

With a deep breath, I reach for the band of his shorts.

He grabs both my wrists in one of his hands. "What the fuck are you doing?"

I stare up at him with pleading eyes. "Let me."

His grip tightens around my wrists as he watches me with narrowed eyes.

"You're on your knees," he says with some sort of awe.

While he's still in his contemplative mode, watching me intently, I release my hand from his and pull down on his shorts.

My breath catches in my throat.

Oh, God.

He's gone commando, and he's already semi-hard.

A tingle crawls down my spine and to my core.

In all honesty, I don't remember how to do this, but I'm hoping my memory will kick in like with my studies and jumping.

I let the shorts fall around his ankles and grip the base of his cock.

A grunt spills from the back of his throat, and I love how his dick jumps to attention at my mere touch.

I affect him as much as he affects me.

Scooting closer, I raise myself up as I give him one long stroke from top to bottom. He doesn't even make an attempt to hide his groan this time.

"Fuck, Reina." His hooded eyes focus down on me.

My heart is on my sleeve as I give him a tentative smile and lick the pre-cum dripping from the crown.

He's throbbing and veiny. I want all of that. I want all of him.

I want him to take me and devour me, but first, I want him to loosen up. I want to change this fucked-up relationship.

If it doesn't change, we'll always be stuck in the middle of nowhere.

I lick him one more time and relish his low groan.

The sound is so masculine and rough, it tightens my stomach.

With one last lick, I take him in my mouth, all the way inside.

"*Fuuuck.*" His fingers thread into my hair, and my eyes close, enjoying the feel of him in my mouth.

Even though I don't remember doing this, apparently I have a knack for it. I don't have to think before I lick the side of his cock. Then I suck on the crown, lapping my tongue over the tip until I taste his pre-cum.

His hips thrust forward and his dick hits the back of my throat. My gag reflex kicks in and I choke on him. Instead of pulling out, Asher keeps it right there. My eyes snap open and I place both hands on his thighs, trying to push him away.

I can't breathe.

I can't freaking breathe.

The look on Asher's face is one of pure contempt. It's like he's planning to choke me to death.

"Did you think you could manipulate me with this?"

I shake my head frantically. The lack of air and the pressure cause tears to blur my vision.

But he's not letting me go.

"That's what you do best, don't you, Reina? You think you can drag me into your web and finish me?"

I shake my head, feeling dizzy and on the verge of fainting.

He pulls back. I cough and sputter, clutching the floor for balance. Drool forms on the side of my face and my chin.

I wheeze for breath like a dying woman with one last wish, like someone who doesn't have anything left.

He wraps my hair around his fist, yanking me up, and I stumble to my feet. I expect him to leave, but he carries me in his strong arms and lays me on the bed on my side.

"W-what?" I ask, confused. My mouth feels dry and empty without his cock.

He kicks his shorts off, tears his T-shirt over his head, and removes his shoes so he's naked.

Fully, absolutely naked.

I stare at his defined abs and a little scar below his ribs. Such a small imperfection makes him even more perfect. The tendrils of his tattoos ripple over his right shoulder and bicep. In the middle of tendrils, there seems to be a sentence in a foreign font. Is that Arabic?

My fingers twitch, yearning to touch those tattoos and ask him what they mean, but before I can think about that, he's on top of me.

His fingers dig into my hips as he pulls my shorts and panties down in one brutal go.

I gasp, the sensation lighting my skin on fire.

No, it's not fire. It's like the air is only filled with him and his presence.

After I woke up in the hospital that day, I struggled with the feeling of belonging and having something—or someone—completely belong to me.

Now, I admit to wanting Asher to be that someone. I want him to belong to me. Talk to me. Touch me.

Maybe that's why his rejection hurts the most.

It hurts to have him hate me so much.

He kneels in front of my face, grasping his hard cock with both hands. "You'll finish what you started."

I gulp, eyeing him carefully. "I thought you said I was manipulating you—why would you want me to finish?"

"Because you'll be doing it on my terms." He pushes the crown against my lips; it's dripping with pre-cum. "Open."

I don't.

If I do, this moment will be over.

Everything will be.

For a second, I just watch him: his perfect abs, the tattoos snaking along his shoulders, and the somber shadow covering his features. It's lust and something else I can't recognize.

He lies down on his side so his cock is in my face and his naked, hard body is glued to my front.

"Open. That. Mouth." There's so much authority in his tone, so much…masculinity.

Sure, I can resist him, but it's completely useless at this point. It's the same as resisting myself, and the meeting with the detective, I can't deal with that.

I part my lips and take him inside, using my hand to direct the pace.

Small sounds slip out from the back of my throat when he lets me bring him to pleasure. This time, he doesn't interfere. He lets me control the pace, sucking him as I see fit.

If possible, he hardens further in my mouth. I can't get enough of having him like this.

I can't get enough of having him all to myself.

Just when I'm about to pick up the pace, a hot wet tongue licks me from the base to the top of my clit.

I gasp around his cock, a full-body shudder going through me.

Holy shit. That feels *so* good.

He does it again, and I clench, thinking I'll come from that sensation alone.

"Who told you to stop?" He speaks against my sensitive folds as his finger teases my entrance.

He thrusts his tongue into my opening, going in and out of me.

My eyes roll to the back of my head. Pleasure hums underneath the surface, threatening to sweep me under.

I battle against the sensation building inside me while trying to suck him as hard and deep as he's doing to me.

His tongue thrusts in and out of me with relentless urgency that turns me boneless. He teases my clit with his thumb, sending jolts of pleasure through me.

"Fuck," he grunts against my hypersensitive skin. "You taste like sweet torture."

My only answer is a moan around his dick. Tingles take over my limbs and I know I'm close…so freaking close.

So I lick and nibble and suck on his cock as hard as I can.

I want to bring him what he brings me.

I want him to be swept away, too.

But most of all, I want him to forgive me.

The wave hits me so suddenly. One moment, I'm getting lost in him, and the next, I'm right in the middle of a storm.

I cry out against his cock, my skin prickling and stiffening. Arousal coats my thighs, and I know he can feel it against his tongue.

The intimacy nearly kills me.

"Break for me," he murmurs against my folds. "Soak me."

His words magnify the force of my orgasm. It goes on and on until I think it won't ever stop.

"Open that mouth wider." He thrusts his hips against my lips, and I do as I'm told.

He pounds a few times before he tenses inside me, and then his cum covers my tongue, my lips, and drips on either side of my mouth and down my neck.

I'm panting, too spent to think or do anything.

Asher isn't done, though.

His cock glides out of my mouth as he pulls me up to face him. We're kneeling on the bed, facing one another.

My eyes are droopy, but I can almost see the change on his face, the slip, the…affection.

Before I can analyze it further, his lips collide with mine in a harsh, punishing kiss.

They're firm and rough, his lips, all-powerful like the rest of him. A rush of desire grips me when I meet his tongue with mine.

He tastes like me.

And I taste just like him.

My fingers thread in his thick strands as I kiss him back with a ferocity that matches mine.

Asher wrenches our lips apart, breathing harshly against my mouth.

"Why the fuck are you kissing me back, Reina?" he breathes against my mouth.

"I'm not supposed to?" I ask, confusion forming a cloud over my head.

"You never do, and you never get on your knees or suck me off." He briefly closes his eyes. "I don't know what the fuck to do with you anymore."

And with that, he grabs his clothes and walks out of the room.

The bitter taste of rejection explodes in my throat, but I don't give in to it. There's still hope.

He'll forgive me.

I will make him.

CHAPTER 24 - REINA

A WEEK PASSES and I'm already adjusting to my position on the team.

It's not easy being a captain. It's a big responsibility, and some of these girls look at me as if I'm their savior or something.

It's not that I have a problem being someone's savior. It's more like I *can't*—not when I don't even know how to save myself.

I'm glad to have Lucy and Naomi with me. Scratch Naomi, she still has that passive-aggressive attitude, but mostly, she's good.

Bree is the one who has been giving me the cold shoulder since the incident in the cafeteria. Whenever I decide something at practice, she doesn't hesitate to point out that we don't do that, that she and the team still remember even if I forgot.

I put her in her place every time. I even had a one-on-one talk with her to tell her to stop challenging my decisions in front of the team.

The squad wants to go to state, and while I didn't care much for that before, now I'm invested in their competitive spirit. Until I find my dream, I'll make theirs come true.

The girls wave on their way out of the shower. I'm late because I had to talk to the football coach about the schedule of the upcoming games.

Next Friday will be the first game I won't watch from afar. I'll be an acting captain who'll be thrown to the top.

To say I'm nervous would be the understatement of the century. I always think I'll trip and fall or do a wrong move and embarrass the entire squad.

No pressure. It's only a home game with a few thousand spectators.

Thousands of people watching.

Yup. No problem falling in front of them. Like, at all.

Lucy is the last to exit the showers.

"I'll wait for you outside," she says while fixing her makeup.

"You don't have to." I remove my shoes. "I'll catch a ride with Asher."

She raises an eyebrow. "Really?"

Never is more like it.

Unless I absolutely have to see him, I don't go near Asher. Since that day he brought me to orgasm; I might have been avoiding the shit out of him.

However, Lucy is having dinner with her dad, and I don't want to keep her. She won't leave if she thinks I don't have a ride.

"So, what's going on between the two of you?" She leans against the locker as I sit on the bench, removing my second shoe.

"Nothing much." I try to be nonchalant, but it's an epic failure.

My body catches fire at the memories of that night.

I might have avoided him, but I watch him whenever he's not paying attention. I watch him work out by the pool, his muscles glistening with sweat and his tendons bulging.

I watch his silence that has a million meanings.

I watch his words that are always precise.

How would it be if things were different? If I hadn't hurt him somehow?

"Luce, how were Asher and I before?"

"Aside from being king and queen?" She laughs.

"Do you really believe we were like that?"

She's silent for a second. "You looked like it from the outside."

"But we weren't on the inside."

She winces.

"Luce…" I stand and look into her eyes imploringly. "Be honest with me. I need to know about my life."

"Well, you know those Hollywood couples?"

"What about them?"

"They're so aesthetically pleasing and look like they have it all, but deep down, they're usually plagued with all types of issues. At the end of the day, most of them are just an image."

Her words strike me deep.

An image.

Why would Asher and I keep up an image? If we didn't want the marriage, I'm sure our fathers would've canceled it.

Why did we choose to be fake instead?

"I'm so sorry, Captain. Are you angry?" She sounds so guilty and apologetic, and it warms my heart.

"Not at all. I asked you to tell me the truth."

She smiles tentatively. "If it's of any value, you two have changed since your accident."

"Even Asher?" I hate the hope in my tone.

"Even Asher." She grins mischievously. "He looks at you differently, you know."

"Differently how?"

"Like he can't wait to get you alone."

I hit her shoulder jokingly. "You're being silly."

She laughs, grabbing her bag. "I mean it. He hasn't been this involved with anything since Arianna's death."

"Wait—Arianna, as in his sister?"

Izzy told me she passed away, but she has refused to tell me anything else no matter how much I probe her. All I know is that Asher's sister died in an accident.

My instinct tells me Arianna's death might explain some things about Asher.

"Yeah," Lucy says.

"What do you know about her?"

"Not much. She didn't belong to our circle. Asher didn't want her to be part of the cheerleading squad."

"Why not?"

She lifts a shoulder. "You're the one who should know that. You were the closest to her."

My mouth hangs open. "I was?"

"Arianna always followed you around like you were her god. You were like best friends—aside from Bree."

Oh.

And I don't remember her.

How can I be so…cruel?

"How about Asher?" I ask, the words strained and choked. "How was his relationship with her? Were they close?"

"More than close. He was like her brother, her mother, and her father all rolled into one. Unlike you, she wasn't popular and didn't have friends, so she relied on the two of you so much. Whenever you sat down, she'd sit with you two. Whenever you went out, she'd go with you like a third wheel. She was kind of clingy, if you ask me."

"Hey," I scold. "She's dead."

"I'm just saying. It must've been a pain to not have your moments with Asher in peace."

"What do you know about her death?"

"Nothing much." She lifts her shoulder. "During our senior year in high school, we all found out she killed herself, and that was it."

"K-killed herself? I thought it was an accident."

Lucy leans closer. "That's what the Carson family has been saying, but you told us back then she killed herself and that it was horrific."

"Did I tell you why she did it?"

"No." Lucy's expression shifts. "Arianna was so lonely, so none of us were surprised she ended her life, you know."

No. I don't know.

Why would a seventeen-year-old kill herself? She had Asher and me—why didn't we help her?

After saying goodbye, Luce slips out the door, leaving me all alone with my jumbled thoughts.

Arianna was so much more than I thought.

She wasn't just Asher's sister; she was my friend, too, and I feel like a failure for forgetting about her and the circumstances of her death.

With those thoughts, I strip and step into the shower.

Water beats down on me, cool and soothing, but my heart won't stop punching so hard against my ribcage.

That gloomy cloud hangs over my head like a sinister promise.

If I don't do something about it, I won't be able to sleep tonight.

A rustle sounds behind the door, and I startle.

"W-who's there?"

The door to the shower swings open and I shriek.

Asher stands at the entrance with a dark look on his face.

MY WORLD TILTS off balance as I stare up into Asher's eyes. Those dark, *dark* eyes.

They're not even looking at me—they're staring right through me.

My body.

My heart.

My soul.

The smarter plan would be to hide from his hungry gaze or kick him out.

I don't.

I continue staring at him as his penetrating gaze trails a path from my face to my breasts and down to my clenched thighs.

It's like his hands are roaming all over my skin, touching me, manhandling me, pulling me closer, crushing me into him.

My lower lip trembles at the mere thought. I'm so glad the water is beating down on me or my reaction to my own imagination would be so obvious.

"You're not supposed to be here," I breathe over the tangible tension in the air.

His eyes finally slide back to my face, the corner of his mouth pulling up in a smirk. "Is that so?"

Is he…flirting right now?

He steps into the shower. He's wearing a black T-shirt and jeans.

I move back. The shower stall is too small to fit us both. He reaches a hand up and I gulp, my heart almost jumping out of my chest.

He flips the knob behind me, turning the water off. I'm all naked and wet while he's fully clothed.

That's unfair.

"What are you doing, Ash?" My voice is just above a murmur.

A part of me thinks he'll douse me with water like he did the other time, but the other part? That part wants him to take me against the wall.

He places a finger on my lips. "Shhh."

The mere contact makes my skin hyperaware of him, everything about him—his presence, that subtle sandalwood scent, the way his hair falls on his forehead.

Everything about him pushes my buttons. I'm so helplessly drawn to him it's becoming stupid.

His thumb skids across my lower lip and I willingly part them. He trails a path to my cheek, leaving tingles in his wake.

It's like he's fascinated with the act of touching me, like he can't believe he's actually doing it.

The thing is, when he thinks I'm not paying attention, Asher watches me, too. Late at night, he stays right under my window as if he can see through the curtains.

He works out near the pool where I always study.

Even if he doesn't have classes, he won't leave campus unless I do.

"You're driving me fucking crazy, prom queen," he growls, gripping me harshly by the nape.

I wrap my arms around his neck. "You drive me crazy, too."

Something flashes in his eyes, something feral and out of control, and then his lips crush to mine.

Asher doesn't kiss; he stakes his claim. It's all passionate and heated like he can't get enough of me, like kissing me is the sole purpose of his existence.

My back hits the wall and I moan into his mouth. I climb up his body, wrapping my legs around his waist.

Even though he's clothed, I can feel the heat radiating off him. It's so similar to the scorching fire going through me.

The passion.

The madness.

It's funny how I used to think Asher was cold. He's certainly not right now.

He's so warm, it's unfair.

"Fuck." He yanks his lips away from mine as if he doesn't want to do this, like it pains him to kiss me.

He doesn't move away, though. His mouth is close to mine as his chest rises and falls with harsh, uneven breaths.

"What the fuck are you doing to me, Reina?"

I'm panting, my starved lungs begging for breath. "I don't know."

"Is that so?" There's no contempt in his tone; it's more like resignation than anything.

"I really don't."

"But I do." He darts his mouth to brush my lips. "Still, I can't stop fucking touching you...can't stop looking at you...can't stop obsessing over you. When one of your asshole teammates lifts you in the air, I want to break their arms."

My heart skips a beat. I didn't know he was watching me *that* closely.

Before I can say anything, his lips go back to feasting on mine. Little noises and moans escape me.

I don't want to stop them.

Or stop him.

He pushes his pelvis against me and his hardness pokes at the sensitive flesh of my thigh.

"Do you see what you fucking do to me?" he grunts before he bites down on my lower lip.

"Ash…"

"It's." *Bite.* "Asher."

"Oh, God."

I rub against his erection, needing friction. Something, anything.

I'm kissing him this time, my fingers pulling at his hair as he keeps me in place by my nape.

"And you're kissing me." He closes his eyes as if he's drunk on the feeling. "Fuck how you kiss me."

I take that as a compliment and push my tongue against the roof of his mouth.

His clutch tightens on my nape, but he doesn't stop me.

He drags his clothed cock up and down my core, dry humping me.

My eyes flutter closed at the sensation. It's like the world only exists in the space between us.

I can feel myself on him even though he's clothed. I can feel how thrusting his hips into me makes him kiss me harder and faster, like this is some sort of race.

My head turns dizzy, but I meet him kiss for kiss, stroke for stroke.

I want him.

God, how I want him.

And it's not only his body. I want his heart.

I want his forgiveness.

I want all of him.

The wave builds in intensity at the bottom of my stomach. It's like a waterfall I'm about to fall over.

He reaches his free hand and twirls a hard, pebbled nipple between his thumb and forefinger.

"Ash…oh…God…"

I come, crying his name out loud. He claims my mouth with his to shut me up.

He kisses me, long and hard like he can't get enough.

He shatters me then gathers me up and puts me back together.

I don't want to stop kissing him, but I need more from him.

So much more.

I reach for his belt with unsteady hands.

"What do you want, prom queen?" he asks with an edge of amusement.

"You, Ash."

"Reina," he growls my name, and I swear his cock thickens even more.

He's about to help me unbuckle his belt when a rustling sound comes from the locker room.

We both freeze.

"Who's there?" I whisper.

Asher places a hand on my mouth. "Shh, if anyone finds us, we'll be suspended."

Right. He's not supposed to be in the girls' locker room, or screwing someone in the showers.

He helps me get down on my feet. When no other sound follows, he opens the door.

"Where are you going?" I can't shake the disappointment out of my voice.

His eyes drag over my body, slow and with purpose. "I'll wait for you at the car."

At the car? He's really leaving me like this?

"We'll finish at home." He winks and steps out.

Oh.

I bite my lower lip at the promise. Maybe this time, I'll convince him to forgive me. Maybe not only will our bodies come together, our hearts will too.

Maybe, just maybe, after all these years of separation, we can find a compromise.

Because I want to be a part of Asher's life.

I finish my shower in record time even though my skin is sensitive and heated because of the orgasm he wrenched out of me.

It doesn't take me long to pull on my jeans, top, and shoes.

I take one last look at the mirror and pause at my flushed cheeks. A smile breaks out on my lips, genuine and...I can almost say...happy.

Happy.

I never thought that word could taste so sweet.

I throw my bag over my shoulder as I push on the door. It's locked.

What?

I pull on it, but it doesn't move.

They can't close now. There are other students still on campus at this time.

The lights flicker before the locker room goes black.

I stop breathing.

No, no.

This can't be happening. Not again.

My pulse spikes as I reach into my bag for my phone. This time, I make sure not to drop it.

I'm trembling all over, my fingers barely able to type anything.

I search for Asher's phone number, but before I can hit it, there's another rustling sound behind me.

I spin around, but it's too late.

My face slams against something hard and my vision goes black.

CHAPTER 26 - G

THIS IS what happens when you don't play by the rules, Reina.

You lose.

CHAPTER 27 - REINA

Hands reach out for me as I run down a dark, filthy alley.

"Rai..."

"Go, Rai."

"Run! You have to go."

My heart thumps louder at that voice. I know that voice.

That voice has been caught between my heart and my ribcage for as long as I can remember.

I've been missing that voice from my life, and it has finally returned.

Reina?

I STARTLE AWAKE, my chest constricting with a frightening force.

"Reina? Are you okay?"

I'm disoriented for a second. It's like I'm still in that alley, battling against the invisible hands coming for me.

It takes me a few blinks to realize I'm home, lying on my bed. Izzy sits beside me, wiping sweat off my forehead.

The back of my throat feels dry and scratchy. "W-what happened?"

Her brows furrow with concern. "Aren't you supposed to tell us that?"

My throat itches as I speak. "What do you mean?"

A look of sympathy covers her features. "Asher found you passed out in the locker room at school."

Memories crush down on my brain. Asher and me in the showers. We agreed to meet outside then...then the lights went off. Something collided with my head and then everything went black.

"Did Asher see what happened?" I ask Izzy.

"I don't think so. He did report it to the administration, though."

Not that they'll do anything. They found no footage the previous two times. This one won't be any different.

My fingers tremble as I pull the sheet up to my chin. The back of my head hurts and something in my body feels sour and beaten up as if I've been running the entire day.

"Where…" I clear my throat from the onslaught of emotions. "Where's Asher?"

"He just stepped out," she says with a tight smile. "He'll be right back."

I try not to feel betrayed that he left me in this state, but an ominous feeling gnaws at my insides.

Something is wrong. Completely wrong.

"There you are." Jason steps into the room, his brows scrunched.

"You're not supposed to be here," Izzy scolds.

"It's fine," I say as he sits on the side of my bed.

Jason is most likely Cloud003, but as I watch his eyes, I don't think he's my attacker.

"Jason!" Izzy hisses. "Stand up."

"I was worried about you." He ignores his mother, his features hardening. "This is getting serious."

"Serious?" I repeat.

He exchanges looks with Izzy, as if getting her permission.

"Don't you dare." Izzy stands over us like the Grim Reaper, glaring down at her son.

"She deserves to know," he says.

"It's not our place to tell her," she argues.

"I deserve to know what?" I stare between them.

Izzy shakes her head frantically.

"Tell me." I pull on the sleeve of Jason's hoodie.

He finally breaks eye contact with his mother and meets mine.

"This incident, the one from the classroom, and even the one on the rooftop were all..." He trails off.

"Were all what?" My voice is as haunted as I feel.

"They're similar to things you dared others to do."

"W-what?"

"I think someone is taking revenge on you, Reina. They're making you pay for what you've done."

I try to breathe, but I can't. Liquid streams down my cheeks, and it's then I realize it's tears.

This...can't be happening.

"It's increasing in intensity," Jason continues. "What if next time—"

Izzy swats him, cutting him off mid-sentence. Before I can urge him to keep going, Asher appears in the doorway.

He glares at how close Jason is sitting to me then narrows his eyes on the tears streaming down my cheeks.

"What are you doing here?" he asks Jason.

"I told him to stay." I sniffle.

Izzy pulls her son by the arm and nods in Asher's direction. "We were just leaving. Get better soon, Reina."

The door closes behind them, leaving Asher and me alone.

He stays at the entrance, watching with a shuttered expression, his thick lashes fluttering down on darkened eyes.

Something in me lightens at seeing him. He's always been there after every atrocity. He's not a white knight per se –black knight is more fitting, but the fact that he's always been there makes my heart race.

He finally strides toward me with both his hands shoved in his pockets. He's changed into sweatpants and a simple white T-shirt that contrasts with his tanned skin and those veiny forearms.

He sits where Jason was and wipes a tear with the pad of his thumb.

"Why are you crying? What did Jason say?"

"He said someone is taking revenge on me. Is that true?"

His jaw tightens, but he doesn't say anything to confirm or deny.

"Why didn't you tell me before?" My lower lip quivers.

His fist clenches, but he continues his silence.

My skin prickles with pent-up energy when he ignores me like this.

"What am I supposed to do now?" I murmur. "How

am I supposed to ask for forgiveness or move forward if I don't know who or what I'm up against?"

"I'm sure they'll show themselves." He wipes the rest of my tears with his thumb.

"What if they don't?"

"You're strong, prom queen. You've escaped them three times, haven't you?"

"How long do you think I can stay strong? What if I'm weak inside?" I sniffle, meeting his gaze. "Would you let me lean on you?"

He pauses at my cheek before he resumes his ministrations. "Why would you want that?"

"I just want to, okay?" I reach over and wrap my arms around his waist, my head resting against his heartbeat. "Don't push me away, Ash."

He stiffens. "It's Asher."

"Whatever, Ash is better." I tighten my hold around his narrow, sculpted waist. My nose nuzzles in his T-shirt and I breathe him in, his sandalwood scent and his warmth. I don't want to be apart from him anymore. I don't want to fight the feelings I've developed for him.

"You're playing with fire, Reina," he says lowly, almost apologetically.

"Then I'll just burn."

It takes him a few seconds before he wraps an arm around my back and pats my head with the other one.

He's hugging me. Asher is *hugging* me.

He pulls me into him and lets me sleep in the curve of his body, my neck hidden in his neck and my legs nestled between his.

"Just sleep," he murmurs against my head, planting a chaste kiss on top.

As I close my eyes, I know I'll sleep the best I have in ages.

Because I finally feel like I belong.

"We'll be together forever?"

Her hand lies on my chest, where my heart beats loud, tears welling in her eyes. "Even if I'm not here in person, I'll always be here, Rai."

I nod several times and hold on to her hand like it's the only line I have in life. "You'll be okay, Rei."

She smiles, her nose twitching a little. "No. We will be okay."

When I speak, my voice is barely a whisper, "I love you, Reina."

"Love you, too, Rai."

MY EYES SHOOT open to be greeted by the darkness.

Deep, uncontrollable darkness.

I open my mouth to shriek, but no sound comes out.

A heavy weight settles on my chest, shifting as if about to burst through.

That's when I realize I'm not breathing. Nothing is suffocating my air, so why the hell am I not breathing?

Breathe.

Breathe.

"Reina!"

My lungs kick into gear at that voice. That low, firm voice with the slight huskiness.

A light illuminates the room and with it, my lungs regain their functions. I gasp for air as if I were drowning and now I'm finally seeing the surface.

Strong arms hold me in a steel-like cage as I breathe in and out.

Inhale. Exhale.

Sandalwood and citrus.

Asher.

My nails dig into the thin material of his T-shirt as I stare up at him. Blurriness still clouds my vision from the tears in the dream—or memory.

He watches me with an indecipherable expression. His thick brows furrow downward as his thumb strokes the skin of my belly where my top meets my shorts.

Up and down. Up and down.

The friction his touch creates is like a soothing lullaby. A reason to breathe. To remain here.

Asher must've showered because his hair is half damp, falling over his forehead in a perfect mess. With the bedside lamp on, the green of his eyes flickers to a darker color like the night or... the unknown.

Why do I keep gravitating toward the unknown? Is it the thrill? The feeling of having my will taken away?

True, that unknown keeps the gloomy cloud at bay. Asher's presence, although not always pleasant, has been an anchor.

Something I can lean on, something I can watch and breathe.

"What was it?" he asks in that suspicious tone that he's been using with me since I woke up in the hospital.

It's like I breathe and he suspects I have an ulterior motive behind that.

"Reina."

One word. It's just one word, my name, but he says it with so much authority, so much power, my thighs quiver.

How would it feel like if he used that voice while he's inside me and —

I internally shake my head. That's a totally wrong image at this time.

"It was..." My voice comes out hoarse as if I've been shrieking at the top of my lungs. I clear my throat. "Just a dream."

"What kind of dream?" His piercing gaze remains the same, hard and unyielding.

He's not letting this go.

I lean my head further so it lies on his solid shoulder and I get a complete view of his features. Something has changed about them, they're almost... softening.

There's no trace of the Asher who only looked at me with pure hatred.

"It's not important," I say.

"Tell me and I'll decide whether it's important or not."

"It doesn't make sense, okay?" I sigh. "I was calling someone else Reina. It's obviously some play of my subconscious."

"Play of your subconscious," he repeats with a neutral tone as if he's feeling the words or trying to figure out why I said them.

His expression remains sealed for the most part, but his grip around me tightens a little. "What else happened?"

"The voice called me Rai and we promised each other things... I don't know. I told you. It doesn't make sense."

"Have you had such dreams before?"

"Yeah. A few times." I pause, squinting at the

distance. "Now that I think about it, it was always like I was talking to myself."

"Talking to yourself. Interesting."

"Why? What do you think happened?"

The calculating streak rushes back to his features. "I'm piecing it together myself."

"It doesn't make sense, what's there to piece?"

"Is that what you really think?"

I swallow the lump at the back of my throat. "I... don't know."

And I don't *want* to know. Those dreams must be some cruel joke from my subconscious. Otherwise, things will turn for the worst.

That could mean I have a dissociative personality disorder or something. That's the only explanation for the fact I talk to myself and have two names for me.

There's also the possibility of a twin, but it's null and void. I've been an only child my entire life.

The up and down of Asher's thumb on my hip stops for a second before resuming.

My heart picks up speed the more he touches me. I'm drowning in him. In his aftershave with that light citrus, masculine scent. In the warmth of his embrace.

How could he become so warm after he was so cold?

What changed?

"Why are you here, Ash?" I ask in a low tone.

"It's Asher," I swear he stopped himself from rolling his eyes. "And you were crying last night, remember? You kind of clung to me."

"You could've left when I was asleep. Actually, you did. You had a shower and a change of clothes. So why did you come back?"

He's silent for a few seconds, the air stretching with unsaid words, before a deep sigh rips from him. "Go back to sleep, Reina."

I dig my fingers harder into his chest. "No. Tell me. If you hate me so much, why do you keep coming back to me?"

His silence war returns and I expect him to shut me off, to pretend we never had this conversation.

Hell, I expect him to get up and walk out of the room. Sure, I should've had what I could get from Asher. I should've probably kept my mouth shut and slept in his embrace and pretended nothing happened.

But I owe myself so much more than that.

True, Old Reina was a devil's spawn and she hurt Asher in some way, but I'm not her anymore. If he can't see that, if he can't differentiate between the two of us, then he doesn't deserve the new me.

Instead of pushing me off and walking away,

Asher's jaw clenches and his eyes find mine. They're green, raw, and…confused?

"I don't know."

"You don't?" I whisper as I feel his words hitting a deep, secret part of me.

A part I thought was sealed and protected.

A part I thought Asher would never reach.

How could his mere words open the gates to my armored heart? How could I let him touch me so deeply?

Am I too far gone?

Asher flips me over and I land underneath him with a gasp. His massive body hovers over me as his thighs cage mine and one of his hands prisons both my wrists above my head on the pillow.

My heart rate picks up and a strange sensation claws at the bottom of my stomach. No, not strange. That sensation is exclusive to Asher. Whenever he's in view, whenever he's in my immediate vicinity, that need to fuse myself with him grips my being and refuses to let go.

He's tenacious that way, Asher.

He broke me in a whole different way than he initially planned. He was after my spirit, he got my heart.

My stupid, fluttering heart.

"Yes, Reina. I don't know why the fuck I can't stop thinking about your laugh and your smile. I don't know why I keep watching you all the time. I don't know why my dick only comes to life when you're around." He strokes his thumb along my jaw, keeping me pinned in place. "So why don't you tell me? What type of fucking game are you playing this time?"

With every word out of his mouth, my chest flutters and my thighs become slick with arousal.

Softening my tone, I whisper. "No games. It's me. Just me."

"Just you."

"Just me."

"Even if I say you're mine now?"

I smile despite myself. Deep down, I think I knew I belonged with Asher since the time I woke up in the hospital. I guess I was just too proud to admit it back then.

I fought it. God, I fought it *so* much, but the answer has always been tucked in the darkest pits of my soul.

"Yes," I murmur.

Asher rolls his hips, lowering himself to me. An unmistakable erection nestles between my thighs, hard and ready. "Say you're mine."

"I'm yours." It's the easiest words I had to say.

A groan rips from the back of his throat as he slams

his lips to mine. The ferocity of his passion ignites my own and I have no choice but to kiss him back, get lost in his hard mouth and the unspoken words he's telling me with his lips.

How much he loves I'm his.

How much it drives him insane.

How much he wants *me*.

They're all a translation of my own emotions. Asher and I might not see eye to eye on everything, but right now? Right now, our lips and tongues are doing all the talking.

His grip on my wrists hardens as he angles my head with his free hand to kiss me thoroughly. Asher isn't interested in a mere kiss. He wants to conquer me whole so there's no part of me left for the taking.

So every inch of my being belongs to him.

He releases my wrists so he can pull my top and sports bra over my head. When it tangles against my hair, he rips the top off.

The power in his strong hands and the unrestrained desire in his eyes cause me to pant.

No. Not mere desire.

That look is so predatory like he's been waiting a long time for this moment.

Maybe I've been waiting for it, too.

His fingers dig into the tender flesh of my breasts.

My nipples pucker into tight nubs as he runs his thumbs over them. The friction shoots straight between my legs.

Oh, God. This is pure torture.

His ferocious gaze slides from my nipples to my face that must be all flushed and red. "These tits are mine, too, aren't they?"

I nod.

He pinches one between his fingers and I hiss a breath at the pleasure mixed with pain. "Does it hurt, prom queen?"

I bite my lower lip to cage the whimper trying to escape.

He leans over and bites the other nipple into his mouth, nibbling on it. "Answer. Me."

"Yes…it does," I pant.

"Do you hate it?" His slight scruff scratches against the sensitive skin of my breasts.

"N-no."

He lifts his head, a grin tilting his lips. "No?"

I must be out of my mind because all I can do is shake my head. I don't know what it is about Asher's roughness that draws me in, but it's there.

Like being carried away in a current. Like free-falling in a waterfall.

There's something liberating about this type of pleasure mixed with pain.

Something like being…alive.

It's like that gasp of air after drowning, the first breath after being reborn.

He releases my breasts so he can hook his fingers on the waistband of my shorts. "If I reach under these, will I find evidence?"

Goosebumps erupt on my skin as his knuckles drag down my overheated thighs. He throws my shorts and panties somewhere behind him.

He thrusts a hand between my naked thighs and dips a finger against my slick folds.

"Fuck." He grunts. "You're soaked."

My trembling thighs willingly part for him as he slides his finger up and down my slit. He teases me with such ease, as if he knows my body more than I do.

His lean, rough digits are enough to start a low humming at the bottom of my stomach. The sensation alone nearly pushes me off the edge.

"Is this for me, prom queen?"

I look away, my cheeks flaming. It's not due to embarrassment, but rather… arousal. I don't want him to see my face right now or how much of an effect he has on me.

He tsks, a tinge of darkness in his tone. "That's not how it works. Look at me."

I don't.

He thrusts a finger inside me and my back arches off the bed as my walls clench around his digit. "I said. Look. At. Me."

Taking a deep breath, I slowly face him. I'm panting, my face heating like a pit of fire. My hair sticks to my temples with sweat and my lips are parted with the need for more.

So much more.

"When I order, you obey. When I ask, you fucking answer. That's the only way this will go, got it?"

A sense of Déjà-vu hits me out of nowhere as I nod once.

"Open that mouth."

I do. I just...do. My lips fall open, tingling with anticipation.

With his finger still inside me, Asher thrusts his free thumb between my lips. "Suck, like you mean it."

I wrap my lips around his digit and keep eye contact as I lap on the skin with my tongue. He tastes fresh and masculine. My thighs clench around his other hand, begging for more.

He pulls back his thumb, and I pant as he presses it at my bottom lip.

"Now, answer me." He works his finger inside me in an increasing rhythm. "Are you wet for me?"

Oh, God. Why does he have to say that with that extremely authoritative tone? I can't resist that tone even if I tried to.

"Yes," I murmur.

"I didn't hear that." He thrusts another finger, pounding both of them with a maddening urgency.

"Oh...oh..." My back lifts off the mattress as the wave hits me. It's slow at first, too slow I barely feel it coming.

Then it slams into me in one go like that free fall from the waterfall. Like being caught in the eye of a storm.

"Say it, Reina," he orders against my ear.

"You...it's for you. Only you."

"That's my prom queen." He claims my lips in an all-consuming kiss as the wave pushes me left and right. It takes me high, just to drop me back down again.

When I come down, he's watching me with a hardened gaze, so consuming and...uncut. He's not hiding any of his emotions right now.

He's all bare.

If I were a better judge of feelings or not caught in the orgasm halo, I could've probably read those emotions.

I could've probably had something to go with.

But I don't.

My chest rises and falls at a frightening speed. With each inhale, my nipples brush against his T-shirt, hardening even more.

I lie completely naked underneath him while he remains clothed. That's not how it's supposed to go.

Hooking my trembling fingers on either side of his T-shirt, I pull it over his head.

He lets me, but he's watching me with a guarded expression. The uncut version is gone and his suspicious self is back on.

I hate it when he hides from me, when he builds forts and summons guards, when he calculates his every movement.

Soon, he won't.

I'll get under his skin as deep as he got beneath mine and he won't be able to hide anything from me.

"What are you doing, prom queen?" His hands fist on either side of him as if he's stopping himself from doing something.

"Making things fair." I meet his gaze with my imploring one as I throw the T-shirt away.

"You never undressed me before."

"I'll fix that from now on." I lean over and grab the

waistband of his sweatpants and drag them down his legs.

His hard cock springs free of its confinements, and I get caught eyeing it. Asher grunts as I watch it. Almost as if he's feeling me touch it.

"Fuck, Reina." He kicks the sweatpants away and slams me back against the bed. "For the last goddamn time, what's your game?"

"You," I whisper.

"Reina," he growls, impatience slipping into his tone. His dick twitches between my thighs, his impatience matching my own.

My fingertips touch the corner of his mouth. "It's always been you."

He pauses. I pause, too, realizing the weight of my words.

It's always been you.

How long are we talking about? Since I regained my memories? Or does it go way back?

Asher doesn't allow me or himself to think about it.

He wraps a hand around my throat. It's not tight to cut off my breathing, but it's firm enough to keep me from moving. It's firm enough to translate his dominance.

If it were another person, I would've asked him to use protection, but it feels wrong with Asher. Besides,

I'm on the shot. I checked during one of my visits to the hospital, because maybe I've been thinking about sex with Asher for some time now.

"You're well and truly fucked, prom queen."

"Why?" I strain to say the words.

"Because you're mine now," he growls as he thrusts inside me in one go.

My body feels like it's burning from the inside out. Not only that, but my heart beats so loud, if it doesn't cause me a heart arrest now, I don't know when it will.

The world halts for a beat.

Asher is filling me whole and erasing everything else from our vicinity.

My gaze collides with his in that pause. For a moment, as our bodies join, our spirits join, too.

We become one.

He starts rolling his hips slowly, drawing goosebumps over the already formed goosebumps. Perspiration trickles down my temples as I watch him. His hard gaze and his straight nose. His sharp jaw and his kissable lips. His ragged breathing and his solid abs.

How could I not fight for him before? How could I ever hurt him?

Just when I'm falling into the slow rhythm, he fastens his pace. He pounds into me with the renowned energy of a dying man finding refuge.

It's like he's also been drowning and is now coming up for air, too.

I wind my hands around his forearm that's holding onto my throat. I hang on to him as he hangs onto me.

And I let go.

I melt in his dominance and his masculine force, in his ruthless power and maddening energy.

The roll of his hips becomes harder and faster. My body arches off the bed as he owns every inch of my soul and something else I'm too scared to admit.

"Ash…"

"What? Tell me." The rumble of his voice intensifies the pleasure whirling inside me.

"I…I'm…"

"Close?" He licks my lower lip as he tightens his grip around my neck.

I nod frantically.

"You'll come all over my dick because you're mine. Only mine."

I nod again, my throat closing in with the violence of the wave about to hit me.

"Say the words, Reina."

"Y-yours." My voice cracks. "Only yours."

"Fuck!" His body grows tense as spurts of his cum coat my insides.

My body trembles with the force of his release and the wildness of my own.

My mouth stays open in a wordless 'O' as multiple bursts of pleasure hit my womb and shoot through my entire body.

Or rather, past my body and into my soul.

My eyes flutter closed as my head rolls back against the pillow. His hold against my throat only heightens the sensation.

It takes me several minutes to come down from the high, to catch my breath.

To actually *breathe.*

Why the hell have I waited this long to do this?

When I open my eyes, I find Asher watching me with intensity but also…affection and something else.

Something so sinister and tangible, I nearly taste it on my tongue.

Before I can get a better read of his expression, he releases my throat and crawls on top of me, his knees settle on either side of my face. He grabs his semi-hard cock in his fist and stares down at me. "You know what to do."

"I…do?" I whisper, staring between him and his dick. "What am I—?"

"Shh, don't talk. Use that mouth for something else."

Does he want me to get him off? Didn't he just come inside me? The evidence is still dripping between my thighs.

Still, I let my lips fall open and take him inside. He tastes like...me. Oh, God. This is a lot more intimate than I thought it would be.

A grunt spills from Asher's throat as he strokes my hair back. "Do you taste us, prom queen?"

I nod, my cheeks flaming, as I lick him more diligently.

His fingers trail from my hair to the hollow of my cheek. "Fucking blushing."

He doesn't sound happy as he says it; if anything, he appears a bit mad? But why? Why is he angry that I'm blushing?

"I don't know what the fuck to do with you anymore." He pulls out of my mouth, and a sense of emptiness engulfs me.

I expect him to leave, like that time after the first orgasm both of us had together.

The gloomy cloud is looming in the distance, waiting to swallow me.

Asher gets off me, and a tightness grips my throat, a sense of rejection, of...nothingness.

No. I don't want to be alone right now.

I'm about to step on my pride and ask him to stay.

I'm about to clutch his arm and hold him to me, but he does something unexpected.

Asher lies on his back and pulls me to the curve of his body by the arm. My head rests on his chest where lines of his tattoos cover his shoulder; tattoos I still don't know the meaning of.

The sense of abandonment withers away as infuriating tears of gratitude fill my eyes.

He's...staying of his own volition.

"Ash..."

"Sleep, Reina. Tomorrow is a big day."

I want to ask what for, but I don't have the energy, so I close my eyes and do as he said.

I sleep.

IN THE MORNING, I wake up to an empty bed.

Asher's scent is all over my pillows and me, but he's nowhere to be seen.

He probably retreated back to his room so no one would see us.

Still, it feels empty to wake up to this cold after last night's warmth. There's a sweet ache between my legs every time I move and it brings back memories of how he owned me.

I dress in a cute navy dress and take extra time to do my makeup.

I want to knock Asher off his feet. I want him to look at me like he did in the shower yesterday, like he did when he fucked me and when held me as I fell asleep.

He'll forgive me.

I can feel it in my bones now.

I already cracked his armor, and I have to keep going to destroy it all.

When I come downstairs, I'm hit by the gloomy energy in the house.

The usual pop songs Izzy fills the kitchen with are absent. There are no flowers in the living area. Jason isn't practicing in the backyard. Asher isn't doing push-ups by the pool.

The house is eerie and quiet, like a cemetery.

I tiptoe around the kitchen, searching for Izzy. Instead, I find Jason drinking milk from a huge cup.

"Morning." I grab a bowl for cereal. "Where's Izzy?"

"Preparing roses for the anniversary."

I slide in at the counter beside him. "What anniversary?"

He meets my gaze over his cup. "Arianna's death. This is the third anniversary."

Oh.

That explains the funeral-like atmosphere in the house.

"Are Alex and Asher going to the cemetery?" I ask.

"If you're thinking about going with them, it's better if you don't."

I pause pouring cereal into the bowl. "Why not? Arianna and I were friends."

He raises an eyebrow. "Were you?"

"What is that supposed to mean, Jason?"

"You weren't friends."

"But Lucy said we—"

"Lucy doesn't live in the same house as you." He puts the bottle of milk on the counter. "Arianna ruined your life, Reina, and you didn't sit still."

My hand trembles around the box of cereal. "I…I didn't sit still?"

"Remember when I told you yesterday that someone is getting revenge?"

I release the box and face him. "What about that?"

"The biggest sin you committed might come back to haunt you."

"I don't know what you're talking about." My legs shake, but I stand up anyway.

An urge pushes me to get out of here. I don't want to stay with Jason or hear whatever nonsense he's spouting.

His eyes droop on the sides. "You drove Arianna to suicide, Reina."

"No…" I'm stepping backward, tears gathering in my eyes. My back hits a chair and I stumble, almost falling to my face.

"And do you know who has the biggest grudge against you because of that?" he continues in that clear, neutral tone.

"I don't want to hear it!" I shout, my voice plagued by tremors.

I turn around and run. My bag falls, books, pens, and notebooks scattering, but I don't pay it attention.

I need to get the fuck out of here.

"It's Asher!" Jason shouts at my back. "He returned for revenge, Reina."

I didn't hear that.

I didn't hear him say those words.

My legs turn rigid, but I don't stop running. I don't even know where I'm going. This could be the back-yard or the pool.

I don't stop to look behind me or to think.

This can't be true.

This can't be happening.

Asher isn't taking revenge on me. Jason has every-thing mixed up.

He's Cloud003. He doesn't want what's best for me.

He's *lying*.

The sound of a familiar voice stops me in my tracks. I'm in the backyard near the garage.

I tiptoe toward that voice, my heart bleeding and ripping to pieces.

Asher crouches in front of a stone painted with faded pink. He's wearing a suit, sharp and black. His jet black hair is combed back.

I hide behind a tree, gripping it with trembling fingers.

"It won't be long now, Ari," he says to the stone. "I'll make Reina pay for what she did to you even if it's the last thing I do."

I stumble and fall on my ass.

Flashbacks of what happened in the last couple of weeks assault me.

The rooftop, the classroom, and—last but not least —yesterday.

Asher wasn't there to save me.

He orchestrated the entire thing.

CHAPTER 30 - G

TIME FOR THE GRAND FINALE.

TO BE CONTINUED.
The story continues in the final part,
All The Truths.

WHAT'S NEXT?

Thank you so much for reading *All The Lies*! If you liked it, please leave a review! Your support means the world to me.

You can read Asher friend's story in Deviant King.

Next up is the second part of the duet and the conclusion of Asher and Reina's story, All The Truths.

BLURB

The truth doesn't set you free.

Revenge shouldn't be rushed. It needs to be savored.

Reina ruined my life and it's only fair I ruin hers back.

Or that was the plan.

That was before she got under my skin and flowed into my blood.

Life as we know it crashes and burns.

All we have left is revenge.

Or is it?

ALSO BY RINA KENT

For more titles by the author and an
explicit reading order, please visit:
www.rinakent.com/books

ABOUT THE AUTHOR

Rina Kent is an international bestselling author of everything enemies to lovers romance.

Darkness is her playground, suspense is her best friend, and twists are her brain's food. However, she likes to think she's a romantic at heart in some way, so don't kill her hopes just yet.

Her heroes are anti-heroes and villains because she was always the weirdo who fell in love with the guys no one roots for. Her books are sprinkled with a touch of mystery, a healthy dose of angst, a pinch of violence, and lots of intense passion.

Rina spends her private days in a peaceful town in North Africa daydreaming about the next plot idea or laughing like an evil mastermind when those ideas come together.

If you're in the mood to stalk me:

Website: www.rinakent.com

Neswsletter: www.subscribepage.com/rinakent

BookBub: www.bookbub.com/profile/rina-kent

Amazon: www.amazon.com/Rina-Kent/e/B07MM54G22

Goodreads: www.goodreads.com/author/show/18697906.
Rina_Kent

Instagram: www.instagram.com/author_rina

Facebook: www.facebook.com/rinaakent

Reader Group: www.facebook.com/groups/rinakent.club

Pinterest: www.pinterest.co.uk/AuthorRina/boards

Tiktok: www.tiktok.com/@rina.kent

Twitter: twitter.com/AuthorRina

Made in the USA
Middletown, DE
24 November 2022

15931488R00172